HAMMER TIME

"No talking from here on out unless I say so," Fargo said.

"Whatever you say, scout," Barstow said with ill-concealed contempt. "But just so you know, if any mangy redskins try to lift our scalps, we're killing as many of the vermin as we can, whether you like it or not."

Fargo drew rein and waited for Barstow to come up next to him. "I'm not your captain," he said.

"What's that supposed to mean?"

"When I tell you not to talk, I mean it." Fargo drew his Colt as he spoke and slammed the barrel against Barstow's temple with enough force to cause the private to reel in the saddle, but not knock him out. "Have anything else to say?"

His eyes fiery pits of spite, Barstow motioned that he did not.

"Keep it that way." Fargo twirled the Colt into its holster and flicked his reins. Then he heard the sharp *click* of a gun hammer. . . .

THE
TRAILSMAN
#303

TERROR
TRACKDOWN

by

Jon Sharpe

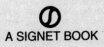

A SIGNET BOOK

SIGNET
Published by New American Library, a division of
Penguin Group (USA) Inc., 375 Hudson Street,
New York, New York 10014, USA
Penguin Group (Canada), 90 Eglinton Avenue East, Suite 700, Toronto,
Ontario M4P 2Y3, Canada (a division of Pearson Penguin Canada Inc.)
Penguin Books Ltd., 80 Strand, London WC2R 0RL, England
Penguin Ireland, 25 St. Stephen's Green, Dublin 2,
Ireland (a division of Penguin Books Ltd.)
Penguin Group (Australia), 250 Camberwell Road, Camberwell, Victoria 3124,
Australia (a division of Pearson Australia Group Pty. Ltd.)
Penguin Books India Pvt. Ltd., 11 Community Centre, Panchsheel Park,
New Delhi - 110 017, India
Penguin Group (NZ), cnr Airborne and Rosedale Roads, Albany,
Auckland 1310, New Zealand (a division of Pearson New Zealand Ltd.)
Penguin Books (South Africa) (Pty.) Ltd., 24 Sturdee Avenue,
Rosebank, Johannesburg 2196, South Africa

Penguin Books Ltd., Registered Offices:
80 Strand, London WC2R 0RL, England

First published by Signet, an imprint of New American Library,
a division of Penguin Group (USA) Inc.

First Printing, January 2007
10 9 8 7 6 5 4 3 2 1

The first chapter of this book previously appeared in *Black Rock Pass,* the
three hundred second volume in this series.

Copyright © Penguin Group (USA) Inc., 2007
All rights reserved

Ⓡ REGISTERED TRADEMARK—MARCA REGISTRADA

Printed in the United States of America

The Trailsman

Beginnings . . . they bend the tree and they mark the man. Skye Fargo was born when he was eighteen. Terror was his midwife, vengeance his first cry. Killing spawned Skye Fargo, ruthless, cold-blooded murder. Out of the acrid smoke of gunpowder still hanging in the air, he rose, cried out a promise never forgotten.

The Trailsman they began to call him all across the West: searcher, scout, hunter, the man who could see where others only looked, his skills for hire but not his soul, the man who lived each day to the fullest, yet trailed each tomorrow. Skye Fargo, the Trailsman, the seeker who could take the wildness of a land and the wanting of a woman and make them his own.

*The hot summer of 1861—and a
trail of terror that leads from
Montana to Minnesota.*

1

The column of twenty troopers and their pack animals raised more dust than Skye Fargo liked, but it could not be helped. The summer had been dry and the ground was parched. It was part of the reason Fargo had stuck to the Yellowstone River since leaving the geyser country. Without water the soldiers would not last a week.

Except for Captain Preston and Sergeant Hunmeyer, the troopers were as green as grass. Most were boys barely old enough to shave. Most were from east of the Mississippi River and had enlisted in the army to escape the drudgery of farm life or the dull routine of work as a clerk. None had ever been in battle. Few had ever fired a shot at another human being.

They were green, and they were in Fargo's charge, and he would do all he could to ensure that each and every one made it back to Fort Laramie alive.

On this particular morning, Fargo was riding ahead of the column. As their scout it was his responsibility to nose about and be on the watch for anyone or anything that could do the soldiers harm. From his vantage on the crest of a sawtooth ridge, Fargo watched the survey detail parallel the meandering Yellowstone. They were steadily rising toward a pass high on a mountain range that would take them over the range into the next valley.

Finding the pass was foremost on Fargo's mind. He had been through this country before and used the pass a couple of times but it was still no easy task to locate it amid the heavily timbered slopes and crags, even with the knack he had for recollecting landmarks. That was the secret to being a scout. Some men could tell north from south and east from west just by the sun and the stars, but that was not enough. A scout had to possess a memory for landmarks or he might as well be a blacksmith or a banker.

In the wild it was not like in towns or cities, where streets were named or numbered and all a person had to do was remember which was which. In the wild it might be a bald peak or a lightning-scarred tree or a boulder in the shape of a turtle or some other landmark that meant the difference between getting where one wanted to go and wandering around lost.

In this instance, a jagged cliff high on a timbered slope brought a smile to Fargo's chiseled features. He said aloud, "There it is." A big man, broad of shoulder and narrow of hip, he wore buckskins, a wide-brimmed white hat caked with so much dust it was more brown than white, and a red bandana. A Colt was snug in a holster on his right hip. In his boot in an ankle sheath rested an Arkansas toothpick.

Fargo drew rein. He had gone as far as he needed to. He would ride back and tell Captain Preston that if they pushed hard they could be over the pass by nightfall. About to rein around, he happened to glance down. His lake blue eyes narrowed, and he said under his breath, "Damn me for a fool." He had been so intent on the slopes above that he had neglected to notice recent tracks under his very nose. The tracks were of unshod horses moving in single file. A war party, more than likely, not a hunting party, made up of ten warriors. *But from which tribe?* Fargo wondered. The tracks could not tell him that. To the north dwelled the Blackfeet, to the east were the Sioux. To the south roamed the Crows. Farther west were the northern Shoshone and the Bannocks. Or the warriors might be Gros Ventre, or even Ojibway. Of them all, only the Shoshone were outright friendly, the Crows partially so.

It did not bode well. So far Fargo had been able to avoid Indians of any kind, as much for their sake as for the sake of the troopers under his care. He was not a red hater. He did not believe the only good Indian was a dead Indian. Hell, he had lived with Indians on occasion, and rated several as among his best of friends.

Frowning at the discovery, Fargo gigged the Ovaro down the mountain. He figured the war party had passed that way the evening before, heading west. By now they should be miles away and of no threat to the boys in blue. But a sense of unease plagued him all the way to the column.

Captain Preston raised an arm and brought the special detail to a halt. A career soldier, he was in his thirties, and carried himself much like professional soldiers everywhere; stiffly, efficiently, with that everpresent reserve that marked a military man. Preston was not one of those who treated his men as his personal playthings, and had been on the frontier long enough to know that a single mistake in judgment could get them all killed.

Sergeant Hunmeyer, or the Hun, as everyone called him, was another career soldier. Stocky of build, Hunmeyer was immensely strong and immensely disciplined. Captain Preston was in charge but the Hun's will was the glue that held the detail together and molded the troopers into a seamless whole. When Hunmeyer relayed an order, the men jumped to obey.

He did not suffer fools lightly, yet at the same time he was considerate of the fact that his men were inexperienced boys.

"I have good news and not so good news," Fargo announced.

"The not so good news first, then," Captain Preston said. He had a practical bent, and always confronted problems head-on.

Fargo told them about the unshod tracks and mentioned the possible suspects. "If I follow them to their next camp, I can find out which tribe they belong to."

Preston chewed his lower lip, a habit of his when deep in thought. "I would rather you stay with us. Your best guess is good enough for me."

"Either Blackfeet or Bannocks," Fargo said without hesitation.

"Either spell trouble, sir," Sergeant Hunmeyer mentioned, and gazed over his shoulder at the double line of troopers. "I wish we had twice as many men as we do."

"As do I, Sergeant," Captain Preston responded, "but the decision was not mine to make. The colonel figured the fewer of us there are, the better our chances of slipping into these mountains and out again without being seen."

"Let's hope he was right, sir."

Captain Preston sighed. "We have three more sites to check. Let's get on with it. Mr. Fargo, if you would be so kind, stay with us until we are through the pass."

Fargo saw no harm in that. He swung in alongside the officer as the command was given to move out.

After a bit Preston shifted in his saddle and remarked, "It has been weeks since we left Fort Laramie, and in all that time you haven't once mentioned how you feel about the army's plan to build new forts."

Fargo shrugged. "It's not anything I have any control over. Whether I like it or not the forts will be built." The region they were passing through was part of a vast, unorganized territory that stretched from the plains to the Canadian border. Thousands of square miles, largely uninhabited by whites. But it would not stay that way. Lured by cheap land or gold or simply the desire to see a new part of the country, the westward tide would not be denied.

Eventually, settlers would stream into the northern Rockies just as they were already pouring into the mountains to the south. When that happened, they would need protecting. The nearest military posts were Fort Laramie and Fort Bridger, and they were not near enough. So the army had seen fit to send out a special detail under Captain Preston to scout out possible sites for future posts.

Fargo happened to be at Fort Laramie when the order came from Washington, and since he knew the northern mountains better than just about any white man alive, he had been asked to serve as the guide. Now here he was, deep in the dark heart of a land teeming with hostiles, doing his best to see that all of them made it out with their hair attached.

Muttering had broken out among the men, and Fargo could guess why. News of the tracks he had seen was being passed down the line.

"That will be enough chatter back there!" Sergeant Hunmeyer suddenly bellowed. He had a voice that could put the bugling of a bull elk to shame, and was not averse to using it.

The troopers fell silent, but to Fargo the incident was not a good sign. There had been a lot of such muttering of late. Most stemmed from odd little occurrences that had Captain Preston puzzled and Sergeant Hunmeyer riled. Things like cinches that came loose and pitched riders to the ground, or packs coming apart for no reason, or personal items that went missing, and more.

Just the other night, around the campfire, a private named Barstow mentioned that maybe the patrol was jinxed, and heads had bobbed in agreement.

Fargo did not believe in jinxes. But he could not deny that a lot of strange things had happened, and that it was growing worse the farther they went. Three days ago a trooper nearly lost his life when, without warning, his mount began to buck like a bronco. The man had been thrown off and narrowly missed having his skull stove in by a flailing hoof. A burr was found under the trooper's saddle. How it got there was anyone's guess.

As a result of all the goings-on, the men were constantly on edge. They didn't joke and laugh as often as they used to. In the evening they huddled in small groups or sat by themselves, saying little.

Just the night before, Captain Preston had confided to Fargo, "I've never seen anything like this. Morale is low, and there have been a few instances of near insubordination. If this keeps up, I might have to bring a few of the men up on charges when we return to Fort Laramie."

There was little Fargo could do. He knew none of the troopers personally. They tended to keep to themselves, and regarded him as an outsider.

Captain Preston usually called a brief halt at noon to rest the horses but today he deemed it wiser to push on and get through the pass. His decision provoked more muttering.

Fargo was admiring the countryside. Towering peaks, many over ten thousand feet high, reared to the clouds, their slopes mantled in spruce, pine, and fir. Lush meadows rife with colorful wildflowers provided a sunny contrast to the dappled shadows of the heavy timber. Animal sign was everywhere; deer, elk, mountain sheep and mountain goats, wolves, coyotes, foxes, black bears and grizzlies were but a few of the creatures that thrived there.

To Fargo it was paradise. But to many of the younger troopers, raised in the safety and comfort of civilization, the mountains were as alien as the landscape on the moon, and fraught with peril. They were out of their element and they did not like it.

By four o'clock the detail reached the pass, a narrow defile that slashed the mountaintop like a wound left by a giant sword. High rock walls rose on either side, shutting off much of the sunlight.

Fargo was in the lead, his right hand on his hip next to his Colt. He saw no evidence the war party had been through the pass, nor anyone else, for that matter, for many days. He could breathe a little easier. But not for long, as it turned out. No sooner did he reach the end of the pass than he spied gray tendrils rising from the broad valley far below.

"More Indians, I take it," Captain Preston said after Fargo pointed the smoke out and Preston had brought the column to a halt. "Just what we do not need."

"Want Fargo and me to ride down and take a look, sir?" Sergeant Hunmeyer asked.

"Fargo, yes. But not you, Sergeant. I want you here with me." Preston swiveled and pointed at two troopers. "Barstow! Weaver! Up here on the double!"

Their accoutrements clattering and rattling, the pair trotted up and dutifully saluted.

"You will accompany Mr. Fargo. Obey him as you would obey me. Under no circumstances are you to discharge your carbines or your revolvers," Captain Preston instructed them. "Is that understood?"

Private Barstow frowned. He had a round face speckled with freckles and hair that resembled straw. "Begging the captain's pardon, sir, but what if we are attacked?"

7

"See to it that you aren't," Captain Preston said, not entirely in jest.

"But if we are, sir," Private Barstow persisted, "surely we have the right to defend ourselves?"

Sergeant Hunmeyer bristled. "How dare you question the judgment of your superior."

"Now, now," Captain Preston said, wagging a hand. "They are understandably anxious."

"That still doesn't give them the right to balk at an order, sir."

Fargo did not say anything but he agreed with Hunmeyer. In light of the series of minor mishaps and the rising unrest, it was crucial that Preston maintain discipline. Without it, the detail would fall apart.

"We meant no disrespect, sir," Private Barstow said sullenly. "We just want to keep our hides intact, is all."

"As do I," Captain Preston assured him. "So, yes, if you are attacked, you may defend yourselves as Fargo deems necessary."

Barstow did not appreciate when he was well off. "We're to do as the scout wants? We can't make up our own minds?"

In a twinkling, Sergeant Hunmeyer had reined next to him and grabbed hold of Barstow's arm. "You will address the captain as *sir*. He is to be treated with respect at all times."

To Fargo's surprise, the young soldier was not cowed.

"Sure, Sergeant, sure."

For a second Fargo thought Hunmeyer would cuff him. Apparently Captain Preston did, too, because he quickly said, "Enough, gentlemen. To answer your question, Private Barstow, yes, you will abide by whatever Mr. Fargo tells you to do."

Fargo would much rather go by himself but since the captain had made an issue of it, he had no choice.

A jab of his spurs and the Ovaro started down. He held to a walk, every sense primed. Half an hour went by and they were well into the trees when he glanced back at his two young charges. "Stay alert," he cautioned.

"How can you do this for a living?" Private Barstow unexpectedly asked. "Are you insane?"

"It's a job, like any other," Fargo replied, adding, "No talking from here on down unless I say so."

"Whatever you say, scout," Barstow said with ill-concealed contempt. "But just so you know, if any mangy redskins try to lift our scalps, we're killing as many of the vermin as we can, whether you like it or not."

Fargo drew rein and waited for Private Barstow to come up next to him. "I'm not your captain," he said.

"What's that supposed to mean?"

"When I tell you not to talk, I mean it." Fargo drew his Colt as he spoke and slammed the barrel against Barstow's temple with enough force to cause the private to reel in the saddle but not hard enough to knock him out.

Private Weaver was a statue, his mouth agape in disbelief.

"Have anything else to say?" Fargo demanded.

His eyes fiery pits of spite, Barstow motioned that he did not.

"Keep it that way." Fargo twirled the Colt into its holster and flicked his reins. He had made an enemy but he didn't care. Barstow had to learn to obey or he might get them killed. Besides, he doubted the hot-head would be jackass enough to shoot him in the back. But hardly had the thought crossed his mind than he heard the sharp *click* of a gun hammer.

2

Fargo spun. He expected to see Private Barstow pointing a weapon at him, but both young troopers were staring in bewilderment at an unkempt apparition in a heavy bear coat who had materialized out of the undergrowth. The newcomer also wore a beaver hat that had not been washed since the beaver was skinned, and moccasins that fit his feet so loosely that they sagged about his ankles. A salt-and-pepper beard and ruddy red cheeks completed the portrait.

"As I live and breathe!" the big man declared, lowering a Sharps rifle he had trained on them. "Soldier boys! In this neck of creation? It can't be. I must be seeing things."

"We're real enough," Fargo said.

The man tilted his head and arched a bushy eyebrow. "I reckon so, if you can talk and I can hear you. If you talked and I didn't, that would mean my ears were plugged or I was seeing things again, like that time in the desert when I thought I saw a lake but it was sand."

Private Weaver belatedly found his tongue. "You're white!"

"The last I looked in a mirror," the mountain man responded, "but I haven't looked in one in a coon's age so maybe I've changed color and haven't noticed.

Am I purple, maybe? Or pink? I've also liked those two colors."

"He's crazy," Private Weaver remarked.

The man puffed out his ruddy cheeks. "No need for insults, boy. I'm as sane as you or the queen of England."

"See what I mean?" Weaver said.

Fargo swung down. Offering his hand, he introduced himself, saying, "We're part of an army detail sent to scout locations for new posts."

"This far north? The hell you say!" the man declared. "Why, I'll have to travel clear to the North Pole to be shed of people, the way things are going."

It was all Fargo could do not to wince; it was like shaking hands with an iron vise. "What might your handle be?"

"Leslie Mortimer Howard, but folks call me Mountain Joe." Joe chuckled. "I've always been partial to Daisy but I can never get anyone to call me that."

Private Weaver was shaking his head. "Addlepated, I tell you. Touched in the brain and doesn't even know it."

"There you go with the insults again, boy," Mountain Joe said. "Since you're young and don't know any better I'll allow the two to pass, but make a third and I'll eat your toes with my venison tonight."

Private Barstow broke his silence to growl, "Since everyone else is jabbering, I guess I can do the same without being pistol-whipped again." He glared at Fargo. "Shouldn't one of us ride back and tell the captain about this simpleton?"

"Both of you go." Fargo had no use for them anyway. "I'll wait for the column in the valley."

Tugging at his beard, Mountain Joe watched the pair ride off. "I wish I'd known we were going to have company. I'd have put on my Sunday-go-to-meeting clothes." He snickered at his joke.

"We?" Fargo repeated.

"My daughter and me. She's down yonder at our camp." Turning, Mountain Joe put two fingers into his mouth and whistled. Out of the firs came a mule. It walked up to him and nuzzled him affectionately. "This here is Matilda. She's a proper lady, so treat her with respect."

"The mule or your daughter?"

"Both." Mountain Joe stepped into the stirrups of a well-worn saddle. "Come along. I might as well show you the way."

Ordinarily, Fargo shied from prying into another man's affairs but he could not help himself. "How does your daughter feel about living out here in the middle of nowhere?"

"In the middle of Injun country, is what you really mean," Mountain Joe said. "You think it's wrong for her to be out here, and I agree."

"You do?"

"It's too damned dangerous. But have you ever tried to get a female to do something she doesn't want to?" Mountain Joe sighed. "I've tried to get Prissy to go back east more times than I can count. She always refuses, and short of stuffing her in a sack and toting her off, there's not a whole lot I can do."

The forest presently thinned. Just below rose the curling tendrils of smoke.

"You at least should teach her not to advertise you're here," Fargo mentioned, pointing.

Mountain Joe's head snapped up. "Damn! I taught Prissy better than that! We haven't seen hide nor hair of Injuns for weeks, and she's getting careless."

"Your wife isn't with you?" Fargo fished for more information.

"Amelia died giving birth. I loved that gal so much, I wanted to die, too. I put a pistol to my head and cocked it but I couldn't pull the trigger. Prissy needed a parent and I was all she had left."

"How old is your pride and joy?"

"Going on twenty."

Shocked, Fargo said, "Your daughter has lived up in these mountains all this time? You've never taken her to Saint Louis or New Orleans or Denver?"

"Are your ears plugged with wax?" Mountain Joe retorted. "She likes the wilds. She wouldn't live anywhere else."

"But there is more to—" Fargo began.

"Damn, mister," Mountain Joe interrupted, "if you're so all-fired against it, take it up with her. Maybe you can convince her to do what's best because I sure as hell haven't been able to."

A gurgling stream bisected the lush valley, and in a grassy clearing bordering its near bank stood a sturdy lean-to and racks for drying meat.

"We're stocking up," Mountain Joe said. "This valley is a prime spot for elk. We mix the meat with berries and make pemmican, or salt it for jerky."

Fargo had done the same on many occasions. But he was more interested in the woman in a buckskin dress who had emerged from the lean-to.

"That's my girl," Mountain Joe said proudly.

Prissy Howard would turn heads anywhere. A buxom beauty with an hourglass shape and legs that went on forever, she carried herself with catlike grace. A mane of hip-length raven hair cascaded past her slender shoulders. An oval face, a pointed chin, lips as red as cherries, and eyes that sparkled like emeralds added to her allure. She embraced her father, then raked Fargo from head to toe with those emerald eyes of hers. "What have we here, Pa?"

"A scout for the army," Mountain Joe replied, introducing him. "We're about to have a passel of visitors."

The girl offered a sun-bronzed hand that was nonetheless as feminine as the rest of her. "Pleased to make your acquaintance, mister. I'm Priscilla, but I mostly answer to Prissy."

Before Fargo could say anything, Mountain Joe nudged her. "They saw the smoke from your fire, girl. We're lucky they're not redskins or you would spend the rest of your days in some savage's lodge."

"Shucks. I didn't make the fire that big, Pa," Prissy said without taking her gaze off Fargo.

"Big enough." Mountain Joe would not relent. "The next time you make a bonehead mistake like this, I'm taking you to the States to live."

"Like Hades you are," Prissy informed him. "I'm old enough to live where I danged well please, and I danged well please to live with you."

Mountain Joe looked at Fargo. "See what I have to put up with? She's just like her ma. There's no talking sense to her because the words go in her ear and bounce back out. What else am I to do?"

"It's not safe in these mountains," Fargo addressed the beauty. It was not really safe anywhere west of the Mississippi.

Prissy's mouth quirked. "If you're scared, maybe you should go find a general store somewhere, put on an apron, and sell pickles and lady's corsets for a living."

"I was thinking of you."

"Why, I'm flattered. You've known me, what, two minutes, and already you're so smitten, you want to save me from myself?" Prissy laughed heartily.

Fargo felt his ears grow hot. "Go to hell, then. No wonder your father is so worried. You don't have the sense of a goat."

Now it was Mountain Joe who laughed and slapped his leg. "I do declare, daughter! At last you've met a man who doesn't forget he's a man just because you're female."

Prissy's lovely green eyes flashed. "I will not be treated like an infant. I am a grown woman and can do as I damn well please."

Fargo shrugged. "Get yourself killed, or worse if you want. It's nothing to me and never will be."

"That's telling her," Mountain Joe said.

Prissy looked from one to the other and balled her fists. "Pa, I expect you to take my side, not some stranger's."

"I can't when his side is my side, daughter. I've been after you for years to be shed of the mountains but you refuse to heed."

"It would serve you right if I did leave you all alone," Prissy declared. Wheeling, she headed for the lean-to, walking with a stiff-legged gait that showed how mad she was.

Mountain Joe chuckled and jabbed a finger into Fargo's ribs. "She likes you, sonny. I can tell."

"Did a tree fall on your head earlier?"

"What?" Mountain Joe blinked, and chuckled. "Oh. I get it. No, my noggin is fine. But I know my girl, and she wouldn't be so mad at you if she didn't think you were worth a hoot."

Fargo gazed at the mountain they had descended. It would be a while yet before the soldiers arrived. Hooking his thumbs in his gun belt, he ambled over to the lean-to. Prissy was on her knees, hacking at a slab of elk meat with a butcher knife. She did not look up. "You shouldn't be upset. Your father only wants what is best for you."

"No one tells me what I should and shouldn't do," Prissy snapped. "Not even him. And I'll thank you to leave me be. I'm busy."

Fargo leaned against the pole that braced one end of the lean-to. "If you can do as you please, I can do as I please." He grinned and gestured at the meat she was belaboring. "Besides, I've never seen anyone so mad at meat before."

A smile spread across Prissy's lovely features. She stopped chopping and shifted toward him. "No man has ever talked to me the way you did."

"I've seen what's left of women butchered by hostiles. It's not a sight for the squeamish."

"I can take care of myself, thank you very much."

"Those women thought they could do the same, yet they ended up buzzard bait," Fargo noted.

"If all you're going to do is carp, it will be tiresome." Prissy resumed her assault on the haunch.

"How about a truce, then?" Fargo proposed. "Even though you are pretty as can be when your dander is up."

"I am not," Prissy said, suddenly flustered. "I'm as ordinary as dishwater."

"You could take your pick of any gent you meet, and you know it."

Prissy regarded him with new interest. "Does that include you?"

"I won't be ready to settle down until I'm sixty, if then." Fargo's wanderlust was too strong to let him.

"Who said anything about living together and raising sprouts? I'm not ready to settle down, either."

"In that case, I'm male, aren't I?"

Prissy grinned. "That you are. A right handsome specimen, if I do say so myself. I bet you never lack for female company."

Fargo changed the subject. "I saw fresh sign of a war party on the other side of the pass. They were too far away to spot your smoke but I'd be extra careful for a while."

"I'm always extra careful," Prissy said. "It's how we stay alive." She thrust the butcher knife into the meat and left it there. Rising, she gazed fondly at her father, who was busy checking the strips of meat already hung on the racks to dry. "I need to wash my hands," she announced, and made for the stream.

Sensing she had more to say, Fargo trailed after her. He was soon proven right.

"Get this straight. I stay out here because of my pa. He shouldn't be all alone."

"He's a grown man. He can cope," Fargo said.

"I suppose. But what sort of daughter would I be if I didn't stick by his side?" Prissy came to a strip of gravel and, hunkering, dipped her hands in the gurgling water.

Fargo felt a swell of sympathy. She risked her life out of love and devotion. Not every daughter would do that. It said a lot about her character. "He should find a town somewhere he likes and settle down."

"It would be the same as putting him in prison," Prissy said. "My pa has to live free or he will shrivel up and die inside." She wiped her hands on her dress. "You see, we tried it once. He took me to a small settlement on the Platte and we lived there for a month or so. I got by all right. But it was torture for Pa."

Fargo understood. He was a lot like Mountain Joe in that there was only so much civilization he could abide. A week or two of whiskey, cards, and friendly doves was his usual limit. Then he would start to feel hemmed in by more than the walls of his hotel, and light a shuck for the high country.

Prissy was still speaking. "He never complained, mind you. He never once said he was unhappy. But I could see it in his eyes. I could see the life drain out of him bit by bit each day."

"So you pretended you hated it there and made him bring you back to the mountains," Fargo guessed.

"What else could I do? He's my pa."

Their eyes met. Neither spoke. A bond of budding friendship had been established, and perhaps more. Fargo coughed and commented, "It's a damn shame

17

our natures always get in the way of doing what we should."

"Isn't that the truth," Prissy said softly. Shaking herself, she stood. "There are soldiers coming, you say? I suppose I should put a pot of coffee on."

"They have plenty of their own."

"Are you saying you would rather have me to yourself?" Prissy grinned. "This promises to get interesting."

3

The troopers arrived an hour later. Although Captain Preston always insisted on keeping the noise the column made to a minimum, Fargo heard them from a long way off and was waiting in the middle of the clearing when the troopers wound out of the forest and came to a dusty halt.

Preston gave orders that camp was to be pitched fifty yards upstream from the lean-to. As Sergeant Hunmeyer led the detail off, Preston climbed down and shook hands with Mountain Joe.

"There's no reason you and your boys can't camp here with us."

The officer gave Priscilla a pointed look and said mildly, "I'm afraid there is. My men have been deprived of, shall we say, companionship, for almost three weeks. It's best I remove temptation."

Prissy was amused. "Why, Captain, I'm flattered. But you needn't fret on my account. I have a butcher knife I'm not shy about using should any of your men find they can't control themselves."

"I'd rather have them keep all their body parts, if you don't mind," Captain Preston said with a smile. "But you needn't worry. My sergeant keeps a tight rein on things. You will not be bothered. I give you my personal guarantee."

"How long will you be staying here?" Mountain Joe asked.

Fargo was interested in the answer, himself.

"No more than a day or two," Captain Preston said. "We can use the rest. And I would like to impose on your kindness and your familiarity with this territory."

"How's that again?"

Preston gestured. "I take it you know these mountains well?"

"Like the back of my hand," Mountain Joe boasted.

"Then perhaps you would be willing to advise me on possible sites for future forts," Captain Preston said. "Mr. Fargo has suggested a few, but maybe you know of some he doesn't."

It was possible, Fargo admitted. He had a general knowledge of the area but Joe had roamed the region north of the Yellowstone from one end to the other.

"I suppose I might, at that," Mountain Joe agreed, scratching his chin. "But it can wait until later. Right now, why don't you sit and jaw a spell."

"I'm afraid that, too, must wait," Captain Preston said. "I must attend to my men. But I expect you and your daughter at eight for supper. The fare will not be elegant but you won't go hungry."

"Elegant?" Prissy snorted. "Land sakes, mister. Don't put yourself out on my account."

Fargo wanted to stay with the Howards but Preston asked that Skye accompany him, and once they were out of earshot, he slowed and said, "Was there some sort of trouble between you and Private Barstow?"

"Not that I recollect."

"Oh? Private Weaver told Sergeant Hunmeyer that you nearly busted Barstow's skull, to use Weaver's own words."

"I didn't hit him *that* hard."

"Ah. But the fact you felt it necessary suggests to me that Private Barstow was giving you trouble of some kind." Preston held up a hand when Fargo went to speak. "Don't protect him, please. Barstow is the most miserable excuse for a soldier it has been my misfortune to have serve under me. It's not his personal habits. He keeps his uniform and his equipment clean enough, and he doesn't drink. But he's a natural-born malcontent. He complains about everything, and harbors a strong resentment of authority. Why he ever enlisted is beyond me."

Fargo had noticed that Barstow had a surly disposition, but so did a lot of other men he had met in his travels.

"The colonel warned me about him," Captain Preston continued. "He said that Barstow was forever causing problems at the fort. He would get into arguments with the other men. He would balk at having to do work. Those sorts of things."

"I'm not much fond of shoveling horse manure myself," Fargo mentioned.

"That's not the point. I can't let Barstow's behavior go unpunished."

"I'd rather you didn't on my account." Fargo knew some of the other troopers might blame him, and he could do without the ill will.

"I'm afraid I must disappoint you." Captain Preston stopped and regarded the flurry of activity his detail was engaged in. "You're aware of the situation I face, of the petty problems that have plagued us. There's talk of a jinx. The men are uneasy. They gripe and grumble a lot. I must keep them in line or it will only get worse."

"You can do that without involving me," Fargo said.

Preston appeared not to hear him. "Every breach of discipline must be dealt with. Little lapses become big lapses if the men sense weakness. There are hard feelings afterward but they always fade away." He glanced at Fargo. "I would still be on my guard for a while, though, were I you."

Fargo had it, then. All this was for his benefit. Preston was warning him of what might lie in store. "I won't lose any sleep over what Barstow might do, if that's what you're thinking."

"It's not just him. Many of the men are unhappy. They have a lot of pent-up resentment and anger. I wouldn't want them to take it out on you."

"I can take care of myself," Fargo said, and inwardly smiled. Prissy had claimed the very same thing a while ago.

"I'm aware of your reputation, but none of us have eyes in the back of our head." Captain Preston smoothed his jacket and walked on. "Just so you know."

Fargo had what little was left of the afternoon to himself. He stripped his saddle and saddle blanket from the Ovaro and picketed the pinto apart from the rest of the horses, close to where he would bed down. The Blackfeet were notorious horse thieves, and he would be damned if he would make it easy for them.

Captain Preston gave orders that none of the troopers were to leave camp without his express permission. Fargo caught more than a few gazing longingly at the winsome figure a stone's throw away, but no one disobeyed.

Then Preston had Sergeant Hunmeyer fetch Barstow. The private was not in the captain's tent long. When Barstow came out, he was livid. He glared at the world and everyone in it, but especially at Fargo, who had just finished washing at the stream. Barstow went to say something but Sergeant Hunmeyer grabbed the young trooper's arm and propelled him in the other direction.

Word spread in whispers. Captain Preston had put Barstow on camp guard duty until further notice.

From dusk until dawn, Barstow was to patrol the perimeter. If caught sleeping, he would be hauled before a court-martial on formal charges.

As Fargo anticipated, some of the soldiers blamed him. They had heard about the earlier incident from Private Weaver, and put two and two together. Fargo ignored their glares.

Along about six in the evening, Fargo strayed over to the clearing. Mountain Joe was in the lean-to, tamping tobacco into a pipe. "Have a seat," he said, patting the ground. "Prissy is off taking a bath and cleaning her dress. You would think we had been invited to eat with the president."

"Women always like to look their best," Fargo remarked.

"Hell, she never much cared about her looks until you showed up. Now her dress has smudges and her hair isn't clean enough to suit her." Mountain Joe chortled. "Females are the strangest critters on God's green earth, and that's no lie. Prissy's mother, God rest her soul, was one of the strangest. I reckon that's why she hitched herself to a cantankerous cuss like me."

"Females are hard to predict," Fargo agreed. "But they make up for it in other ways."

"That they do, son. That they do. I wouldn't trade my years with Prissy's ma for all the gold in the Rockies." Mountain Joe was quiet a while; then he gruffly declared, "Life's just not fair."

A sentiment with which Fargo wholeheartedly agreed. They talked about the old days when trappers flocked to the mountains after beaver plews and a man could earn more money in a few months than most earned in two or three years.

"I only got in on the tail end of it," Mountain Joe related, "but it was grand while it lasted. Since then I've lived pretty much hand to mouth, but I've never gone hungry nor lacked clothes to wear." He ran a callused hand over his bear coat.

"Aren't you hot in that thing?" Fargo asked.

"No hotter than I would be if I was staked out under a burning sun," Mountain Joe said, and laughed. "You get used to it." Sitting up, he stared at where the stream disappeared around a bend. "It sure is taking that girl a long time to wash behind her ears."

"Did she take a gun with her?" Fargo was thinking of the tracks he had come across.

"Of course. Her rifle. If there was trouble she'd holler or get off a shot." Mountain Joe puffed on his pipe. "Still, it wouldn't hurt to make sure she's all right. You sit tight. I'll only be couple of minutes."

Fargo was already on his feet. "I'll go, if you have no objections." Without waiting for an answer he strode toward the bend. He called out as he neared it in case she was naked, in order not to embarrass her. There was no answer. Stopping, he put a hand to his mouth. "Prissy? Did you hear me?"

Again, no answer.

Fargo wondered if she was farther down the stream. He went around the bend. A long, straight stretch ended at another bend maybe a hundred yards distant. "Prissy?" He hiked along the bank, seeking sign, but found no evidence she had stopped anywhere to bathe. Perplexed, he walked faster. He was almost to the second bend when a low cry fell on his ears. The sort of cry someone might utter if they were gagged or a hand was clamped over their mouth.

Galvanized by concern, Fargo raced forward. He swept around the bend in time to spy a figure in the act of retreating into the woods bearing someone bundled in a blanket. Fargo gave chase. He could not see Prissy's abductor clearly, but he could tell the man wore a uniform.

Prissy wasn't struggling, which did not bode well. Palming his Colt, Fargo flew past several tall pines and snapped off a shot, deliberately shooting high so as not to endanger Prissy.

The soldier dropped her. He did not look back. He did not cry out or resort to a weapon. He simply let go and kept on running, bending low so he was harder to keep track of.

Fargo snapped off another shot. He was wasting lead but he was mad. He came to the sprawled form in the blanket and hesitated. He might be able to catch the soldier. But Prissy wasn't moving and she came first. Thwarted, he knelt. She was completely covered except for her feet and one hand.

"Prissy?" Fargo gripped the top edge and gingerly pulled the blanket lower. She lay facedown, her thick, luxurious hair soaking wet, and not just from water. Blood matted the curls above her left ear, and was trickling down her neck. Fargo probed and discovered a gash several inches long. Her abductor had struck her, and struck her hard. The gash did not appear to be life-threatening, but it was hard to be sure about head wounds.

"Prissy? Can you hear me?" Fargo slowly rolled her over onto her back. The blanket slid lower, exposing her full, firm breasts. Despite the circumstances, Fargo could not avoid stirring low down. He shrugged it off, lifted the blanket, and examined her, front and back. He found no other wounds. Carefully covering her again, he slid his arms under her and carried her toward the stream.

Up near the clearing, Mountain Joe was bellowing like a bull moose. "Prissy! Fargo! Where the blazes are you? What was that shooting?"

"We're here!" Fargo hollered. He went a dozen yards, then lowered Priscilla onto a cushion of grass. Removing his hat, he was about to dip it in the water when the short hairs at the nape of his neck prickled. Instantly, he spun, his hand swooping to his Colt.

No one was there. But Fargo was willing to swear unseen eyes were on him. The eyes of Prissy's abductor.

"Prissy! What's happened to her?"

Mountain Joe was on his knees, his big Sharps beside him, his daughter's head cradled in his lap. "What's this? Blood! By God, there will be hell to pay if someone has hurt my girl!" Reaching out, he grabbed Fargo's wrist. "Who did this?"

"A trooper. I didn't get a good look at his face."

Mountain Joe blazed red from his neck to his hairline. His body shaking with rage, he swore fiercely, then heaved erect. "Bring my rifle! We'll take her to the lean-to and tend her."

Fargo snatched the Sharps off the ground but did not hurry to catch up. He still felt the unseen eyes on his back. He tried telling himself it was his imagination, but the feeling persisted. He stopped, hoping the soldier would give himself away by moving.

"Fargo! Are you coming or not?"

Reluctantly, Fargo headed for the clearing. He had only taken a few strides when he spotted Prissy's buckskin dress. She had hung it over a low limb to dry while she bathed. He snatched it and hurried on.

Mountain Joe had removed his beaver hat and placed it under Prissy's head as a pillow. Now he covered her with his bear coat, then slid the blanket out from under it. Using the butcher knife, he cut a long strip from the blanket. "See that kettle? Fill it with water and hang it on the tripod over the fire." As an afterthought he added, "If you would be so kind."

Fargo was happy to oblige. When he rejoined Joe, the mountain man was staring glumly at his offspring.

"As God is my witness, those soldier boys will pay for harming her. They will pay in guts and blood."

"Only one was to blame," Fargo pointed out.

"They'll turn him over to me, or else."

Fargo had not heard anyone approach. The first inkling he had came when someone cleared their throat.

Captain Preston was outside the lean-to and had not noticed Prissy or the state her father was in. "It's close to eight. I thought I would come over and escort you to my tent personally."

With an inarticulate roar, Mountain Joe hurled himself at the officer.

4

The startled officer was caught flat-footed. He had no chance to dodge or backpedal. The enraged mountain man's thick fingers closed on Captain Preston's throat and gouged deep.

Mountain Joe was beside himself with fury. In his berserk rage over the harm done his daughter, he could easily snap the officers's neck or crush Preston's throat to a mangled pulp.

But even as Mountain Joe sprang, so did Fargo. As Joe's hands clamped onto Preston, Fargo's hands clamped onto Joe's wrists. Mountain Joe was a big man, broad of shoulder and strong as a bull. But Fargo was a big man, too, his shoulders just as wide. And where Mountain Joe's body had grown a bit soft with the passage of years, Fargo was in his prime; his arms were corded with steel sinews, and his midriff resembled a washboard. Mountain Joe had barely begun to squeeze when Fargo wrenched on Joe's arms, tearing them from Preston's neck.

"No! He's not to blame for Prissy!"

Mountain Joe struggled to break free, bellowing, "He's their officer! He has to answer for what they do!"

Captain Preston had stumbled back. Coughing and rubbing his throat, he gazed in confusion from Mountain Joe to Fargo and back again. "What in God's name is this about? Why did you attack me?"

Fargo was holding onto the mountain man for fear of what Joe would do if he let go. "It's his daughter. One of your soldiers tried to carry her off."

"What?" Sheer disbelief etched Preston, to be replaced by budding anger. He came forward and saw Prissy. "Dear God. Who did it? Show me the culprit and I'll see that he spends ten to twenty years in the stockade."

"I don't know who it was," Fargo admitted. "I didn't get a good look at him."

Some of the red had faded from Mountain Joe's face. He stopped resisting and declared, "Whoever it was, they're mine to deal with."

"This is a military matter," Captain Preston said. "I can't have you taking the law into your own hands."

It was the wrong thing to say. Mountain Joe spun and flung out his left foot, seeking to trip Fargo, but Fargo jumped over the out-thrust leg and retained his hold on Joe's wrists.

"Calm down, damn it."

"Like hell!" Mountain Joe fumed.

Just then a small, strained voice intruded. "Pa? Stop acting the fool. You're not doing either of us any good." As pale as snow, Priscilla had revived and was propped on her elbows. "I could use some water. I have a powerful thirst."

Fargo released her father. Mountain Joe's rage had been smothered by a stronger emotion. Scooping up a battered tin cup, Joe ran toward the stream, saying over his shoulder, "You rest easy there, girl."

Prissy lowered her head onto the beaver hat, and winced. Mustering a smile, she said, "I feel like my head was stomped on by a herd of buffalo." She reached up and lightly touched the gash. "How did I get here?"

"That was my doing," Fargo said. "I chased off the man who attacked you."

Captain Preston stepped into the lean-to. He was shaken but had regained much of his composure. "Who did this to you, young lady? I must insist you tell me."

"I would if I could," Prissy said. "But he snuck up on me while I was washing. I heard steps and then a splash. I tried to turn but he walloped me over the head."

Fargo's attention perked. "He jumped in the pool after you?"

Forgetting herself, Prissy nodded, and had to grit her teeth against the pain it provoked. "He sure did. Why? What does it matter?"

"His pants should still be wet," Fargo said, with a meaningful glance at Preston. "If you were to line up all your men—"

"We will know who did it!" the officer excitedly declared. "Come on! We can't waste another second."

"Right behind you," Fargo said. They ran out just as Mountain Joe returned. Fargo felt it best not to explain what they were up to; it might drive Joe into another frenzy.

The troopers were enjoying rare relaxation. The horses had been picketed, a fire had been kindled, and the men were sitting around talking. Sergeant Hunmeyer leaped to his feet at the sight of Preston's angry features and immediately inquired, "Is something wrong, sir?"

"Have the men fall in," Captain Preston sternly commanded.

Although surprised, Hunmeyer was always the professional. Snapping to attention, he did an about-face and duly relayed the order at the top of his lungs.

Equally surprised, the troopers nonetheless scrambled to obey. Shoulder to shoulder, they formed a single row that extended from the picketed horses to Preston's tent, each man as rigid as a board, with his hands at his sides.

Captain Preston started down the line, pausing in front of each trooper to scrutinize their uniforms.

Fargo had already glanced down the line, and was puzzled. None of the soldiers had wet pants. He wondered if it had been possible for the culprit to run back and change into a spare set.

Coming to the last trooper, Captain Preston wheeled. "I only count seventeen. Who is missing?"

"Don't you remember, sir?" Sergeant Hunmeyer said. "Private Barstow is on sentry duty. He's patrolling the perimeter."

Stiffening, Captain Preston shifted right and left. "I don't see him. Where did he get to?"

Hunmeyer pivoted on a boot heel. "Private Barstow, front and center on the double!"

Fargo figured they had their man. Barstow had seen Prissy leave the clearing, and snuck off and followed her. The vision of her nakedness had been too much for him to resist, and Barstow had tried to carry her off and rape her.

"Barstow! Didn't you hear me?" Sergeant Hunmeyer shouted.

Just then the object of their interest came strolling around a thicket to the north, the stock of his carbine cupped in one hand, the barrel across his shoulder. "Hellfire, Sergeant," he said with a smirk, "they heard you clear back in Ohio."

"I said on the double!"

Private Barstow ran the last twenty feet, but he did not run very fast. "Why the fuss? Have those hostiles been spotted?"

Hunmeyer took a step and loomed over the youth like a redwood over a sapling. "You will stand at attention and show proper respect."

"Whatever you want," Barstow said, imitating the rest of the troopers.

Fargo was staring at the troublemaker's pants. They were bone-dry, just like all the rest.

Captain Preston was staring, too. He gazed down the line, then motioned to Fargo and moved past the tent. "Are you sure it was one of my men?"

"As sure as I have ever been about anything."

"But you saw for yourself. None of their uniforms have so much as a drop of water on them." Preston gnawed on his lip. "I don't mean to doubt you but is it at all possible you were mistaken?"

"No," Fargo assured him.

"I don't understand it," Preston said. "The girl was certain, too. Unless the splashing she heard was her own. Maybe she was close to the bank and he pulled her out without getting himself wet."

"That could be," Fargo allowed, although he was inclined to believe Prissy's version. He was about to suggest that the officer go through the saddlebags and bedrolls of every trooper but just then Sergeant Hunmeyer materialized beside them.

"Sir, sorry to interrupt, but I think you should hear this."

"Hear what?"

"Private Barstow, sir. He has a report to make."

Preston strode back. "What is so important, trooper?"

The youth was still at attention, but he appeared bored and answered with a distinct lack of enthusiasm. "I don't think it is, sir. It's the sergeant, here, who insists that I tell you."

His jaw muscles twitching, Captain Preston stood nose to nose with the youth. "I have about reached the end of my patience with you, Private. In case you have forgotten, you are in the United States Army. You will conduct yourself accordingly. That includes treating your superiors as they deserve to be treated."

"I always do, sir," Barstow said with a complete and obvious lack of sincerity.

It made Preston madder. "Your attitude leaves a lot to be desired. From this moment on, young man, I am making it my personal duty to whip you into shape. I will make a soldier out of you whether you want to be one or not."

"Yes, sir," Barstow said, trying hard not to grin.

"Sergeant Hunmeyer says you have a report to make."

"I told him that I thought I saw someone off in the woods but I might have been wrong, sir."

"Be more specific. In order to make informed decisions, I must have precise details."

"I was walking the perimeter, sir, as I was ordered, when I saw something move on the other side of the stream. I figured it was a deer or some other animal, but when I looked closer, I was willing to swear it was a person."

"Did you challenge this intruder as regulations require?"

"No, sir."

"Why not, may I ask?"

"He wasn't bothering us, sir. He was just running through the woods, minding his own business."

Captain Preston cocked his head. "Can it be that you are truly this naive? Was it a white man or an Indian?"

"I honestly couldn't say, sir, although I think it was a white man."

"Was he armed?"

"I didn't notice. Sorry."

One of the nearby soldiers snickered and another

said loud enough to be heard, "There's an idiot for you."

Sergeant Hunmeyer wheeled. "Silence! None of you will speak unless spoken to! Private Stover, I heard that. You will report to me once we are done here so I can refresh your memory about how to conduct yourself in a military manner."

Preston was staring across the stream at the thick undergrowth. "Can it be?" he said more to himself than to any of them. "Is this the explanation?"

"Sir?" Private Barstow said.

"Nothing, Private. You will return to your sentry duty. Sergeant Hunmeyer, assign three more men as sentries, as well. Have one of them stand guard over our horses at all times. The last thing we need is to be stranded afoot."

Fargo was trying to decide whether to believe Barstow. He didn't trust the youth as far as he could throw the Ovaro, but he had to admit Barstow might be telling the truth about seeing someone.

"I must talk to Mountain Joe again," Captain Preston said to him. "In light of the circumstances, perhaps you should accompany me. My throat still hurts from his attempt on my life." Preston waited until they were a third of the way to the clearing to say, "I must ask you again. Is it possible you are mistaken? Could it have been someone other than one of my men?"

"I still think it was," Fargo said. He had to be honest with himself, though. In the shadows, the clothes Prissy's attacker wore might have only appeared to be the same blue as a military uniform. "But I'm human like everyone else. I make mistakes."

"I would dismiss Barstow's claim out of hand were it not for the fact it is just like him not to immediately report what he saw. He is the laziest human on God's green earth. Did you notice how annoyed he was that Sergeant Hunmeyer had told me?" Captain Preston indulged in his lip chewing. "We must be extra vigilant from here on out."

Fargo was surprised to see Prissy up and dressed. She was in the lean-to, on her knees, examining her wound in a mirror she held. Mountain Joe was bent over her, gesturing angrily with the strip he had cut from the blanket.

"Consarn it, girl! You need to let me bandage you. Infection might set in, and then where would you be?"

"The bleeding has stopped. I've cleaned it with hot water. That will suffice," Prissy responded. "Besides, I would look just horrid with that wrapped around my head."

"You can be as pigheaded as your ma sometimes," Mountain Joe growled. "If you weren't full grown, I would take you over my knee and spank the living daylights out of you."

Unruffled, Prissy said, "You would not. You have never, ever laid a hand on me, which is one of the things I've always admired most about you."

Mountain Joe took a step back, his expression almost comical. "Hell in a basket! If there are more contrary critters than females, I have yet to run across them." He turned to stomp off and realized he had visitors. "You again!" he growled at Preston. "Where's the bastard who hurt my girl?"

"I'm still investigating," Captain Preston said. "Have you seen any other white men recently? Or any sign of other white men?"

"What's this?" Joe demanded. "Are you trying to weasel out of the blame? It won't work."

"A sentry thought he saw someone," Captain Preston explained. "I figured that if there are other white men in these parts, you would know."

"Well, there isn't. So your trick won't work."

"It's not a trick. I'm merely trying to ascertain the truth." Preston turned to Prissy. "Tell me again what

35

happened. Maybe there is a detail or two you over-looked the first time."

Mountain Joe moved between them. "Damn your hide. Are you calling my girl a liar? She's told you once and that's enough."

Fargo was ready to intervene if the mountain man lost his temper again. But before that could occur, shouts erupted at the camp, followed by the crack of carbine fire.

Captain Preston jumped to the same conclusion as Fargo. "We are under attack!"

5

The troopers were hunkered behind boulders and trees bordering the stream. Wreaths of gun smoke hung in the air, twisted by the breeze into writhing tentacles.

"Hold your fire!" Sergeant Hunmeyer roared as Fargo and Captain Preston came sprinting up. "Don't shoot unless I say so!"

Ducking low so as not to be an easy target for hot lead or a streaking shaft, Fargo came to the pine Hunmeyer was crouched behind.

"What was all that shooting?" Captain Preston demanded, anxiously glancing right and left. "Are we under attack?"

"No, sir," the sergeant said a trifle sheepishly. "One of the sentries thought he saw something and shot at it. Some of the others rushed to his side, and before I could stop them, they opened fire."

"At what?" Captain Preston wanted to know.

Fargo would swear the sergeant blushed.

"I'm not rightly sure, sir. I didn't see anyone but several of the men swore that they did."

"Which sentry fired first? Was it Private Barstow?"

"No, sir. Private Jones."

"Fetch him."

While they waited, Fargo scanned the woods across the stream. It seemed strange to him that whoever had tried to abduct Prissy would lurk so near the army camp. What did the lurker hope to accomplish? Other than to get shot by a nervous young soldier?

"I don't see anyone over there," Captain Preston remarked, doing as Fargo was doing. "How about you?"

Fargo shook his head.

"I hate to suggest I would doubt your word, but it's looking more and more as if none of my men are to blame for Miss Howard." Preston sounded relieved.

In Fargo's estimation it was too soon to tell. He trusted his senses. He had to. In the wild, indecision could kill a man as dead as anything.

The trooper who returned with Sergeant Hunmeyer was skinny and buck-toothed and barely old enough to shave. "Sir!" he said in a high-pitched voice. "Private Jones reporting as ordered."

"I understand you were the first to discharge your weapon," Captain Preston said in the patient manner of a parent talking to a child. "I would like to know why."

"I thought I saw someone, sir."

"You *thought*?"

"Yes, sir. I was talking to Private Barstow, with my back to the stream, when he suddenly pointed over my shoulder and said that someone was watching us. I turned, and sure enough, someone ducked behind a tree."

"Why did you fire? Was your life threatened?"

"I thought the person I saw had a rifle, sir."

"There's that word again," Captain Preston said dryly. "Very well. What happened after that?"

"Well, Stover and Charley and some of the rest came running up and started shooting."

"Did any of them actually see who they were firing at?"

"You would have to ask them, sir," Private Jones said.

"I have a better idea." Preston turned to Fargo. "This smacks of a job for someone with your experience. Can you slip across and get to the bottom of this mystery?"

"What about all those itchy trigger fingers?" Fargo asked, with a bob of his chin at the ragged line of crouching and kneeling troopers.

"I will have Sergeant Hunmeyer spread word that no one is to fire unless I personally give the order. Will that suffice?"

It would have to. "Give me a minute," Fargo said. Unfurling he ran to where he had left his saddle and saddle roll. Sliding the Henry from its scabbard, he fed a round into the chamber. He loosened the Colt in its holster, then bent at the knees and zigzagged to within spitting distance of the stream. It wasn't deep but it was fifteen to twenty feet across, and he would be in the open every step of the way.

Girding himself, Fargo burst from concealment. In a twinkling he was over the bank and in the water. It rose as high as his ankles, then his knees. A few more steps and it was above his waist. He was intent on the wall of vegetation and not on where he was placing his feet. That proved to be a mistake, for midway across his left foot unexpectedly slipped out from under him. Realizing the bottom abruptly slanted down, Fargo tried to throw himself backward but the water hampered his movements enough so that his right foot, too, began to slip. The next moment he was in a pool up to his chest. Kicking vigorously, he swam the deepest part and in a few yards was able to stand again.

Soaked to the skin, his buckskin dripping, Fargo gained the bank. He did not linger. In several long bounds he was in among the trees and crouched behind a pine. He was mad at himself for blundering into the pool; it was something a greenhorn would do. One of the soldiers had laughed when he floundered and been barked to silence by Sergeant Hunmeyer.

Fargo sidled around the tree to begin his search. He had only taken a few steps when he stopped. His boots were squishing. Since stealth was called for, he sat with his back to the bole and peeled off first his right boot and then his left. Pulling his pant leg down over his ankle sheath, he rose and stalked into the forest. The shadows were lengthening. In an hour the sun would set. He must conduct his search quickly.

Not a sound greeted him, not so much as the peep of a bird or the chitter of a squirrel. Either something or someone was abroad, or the volley the troopers had fired was responsible. Or maybe it was both.

A ghost among shadows, Fargo hugged the available cover. When he needed to, he could move as quietly as an Apache. Always on the lookout for tracks, he paused often to listen. Half an hour of fruitless hunting went by. He figured he had searched long enough and bent his steps toward the spot where he had left his boots.

On the off chance had he might have missed spotting the man's footprints, Fargo glued his gaze to the ground. He paid no attention to the stream, or to the soldiers on the other side. Which proved to be his second mistake of the day. For as he emerged from a stand of saplings, a shout rang out.

"There he is! The one who attacked the girl!"

A carbine boomed and a heavy slug thudded into a tree next to Fargo. He looked up and beheld eight or nine muzzles pointed in his direction. He did the only thing he could. He dived flat as a leaden hailstorm peppered the vegetation. He yelled but the boom of carbines drowned him out.

A dirt geyser kicked up inches from Fargo's face. A tree next to him was struck with a loud *thwack*. Leaves and bits of branches pattered onto his hat and shoulders. Then, as unexpectedly as it had started, the shooting stopped. Angry commands explained why.

"Cease fire! Cease fire, all of you!" Sergeant Hunmeyer roared. "The next man who squeezes a trigger answers to me."

"Fargo, are you all right?" Captain Preston hollered.

Slowly rising onto his knees, Fargo took stock. Other than a clipped whang or two, he had miraculously been spared. He made for his boots and tugged them back on. Avoiding the pool, he waded the stream.

The troopers were standing around looking embarrassed. Most of them, anyway. One who did not was the same one whose shout had nearly led to Fargo being shot to ribbons.

Fargo stalked up to him, and stopped.

"Why are you looking at me like that?" Private Barstow snapped.

"Some people only learn the hard way," Fargo said, and drove the Henry's stock into the pit of Barstow's stomach.

Uttering a sharp bleat of pain, Barstow doubled over. "Bastard!" he hissed, spittle dribbling down his chin. "You had no call to do that!"

"Wrong," Fargo said, and slugged him, a short, swift jab to the jaw that pitched Barstow to his hands and knees. Fargo dearly wanted to hit him again, but he held his temper under control and shouldered past a pair of dumbfounded soldiers.

"Thank God you're all right," Captain Preston.

"No thanks to your men." Fargo knew it was not fair to blame them all for a mistake made by one, but he was in no mood to turn the other cheek.

"I saw it was you," Sergeant Hunmeyer said. "But some of the men began firing before I could order them not to."

"They don't know any better," Captain Preston mentioned. "They don't have enough experience."

Fargo almost slugged him, too. "I'll be with the Howards if you need me," he announced, and kept walking.

"What about the man the sentries saw?" Preston asked. "Did you see any sign of anyone?"

"What do you think?" Fargo retorted. Sergeant Hunmeyer called out to him to wait but he did not stop until he came to the lean-to. A fire crackled, the flames licking at a coffeepot. Prissy was bundled under a blanket, asleep.

Beside her sat Mountain Joe, sadness mirrored in his sun-weathered countenance. "I almost lost her today. I couldn't bear that. She's all I have in this world." He flicked a finger at the coffeepot. "Help yourself."

"Don't mind if I do." Fargo sat with his back to the lean-to so he could keep an eye on the forest on the other side of the stream, and on the camp he had just vacated.

"What was all that shooting and yelling?"

"Some of the soldiers thought I would make a better sieve than a scout," Fargo replied.

"You don't say. It's a good thing most blue coats can't hit the broad side of a stable with a cannon," Mountain Joe remarked. "You should light a shuck. Leave them on their own. Odds are, they'll never make it back to Fort Laramie alive."

"Which is exactly why I can't leave," Fargo said. "I gave my word to their commanding officer."

"Ah." Mountain Joe took a broken branch from a pile and added it to the fire. "I learned long ago never to give my word to idiots, bad men, and mothers-in-law. You end up being bitten on the ass every time."

Fargo chuckled.

"We never do what's good for us, do we?" Mountain Joe lamented. "Take my girl." He gently touched Priscilla's shoulder. "She shouldn't be here. She should live in the States, where it's safe. She should be going to church socials and taking part in sewing circles and such, and be courted by handsome beaus."

"She would rather be with you."

"I know, and until today I've been willing to let her stay because I love her so much, and because I get so damn lonely by myself," Mountain Joe said. "But maybe I'm being selfish. Maybe if I truly love her, I would take steps to do what is best for her whether she likes it or not." He looked up. "I have a favor to ask."

Fargo sensed what was coming. "Why me?"

"Who else? The soldier boys?" Mountain Joe snorted. "The only one worth a damn is the sergeant, but he's chained to his uniform."

"You can trust Hunmeyer."

"I trust you more. There's something about you. Do me this favor and I'll be forever in your debt."

"What is it?"

Mountain Joe bowed his shaggy head low over his daughter. "Take her away. Get her to civilization where she belongs. Help me give her a chance at a normal life."

Fargo could imagine her reaction. "Shouldn't that be her choice to make?"

"I used to think so but not any more. I should have sent her off years ago, when she was knee-high to a fawn. But it's never too late to remedy a mistake." Emotion choked Joe's voice. "I have some money. It's not much but it should last her a month or two. She can find a job, get a place to live. In time she'll marry and have sprouts and live happily ever after."

"Life isn't a fairy tale."

"True. But it doesn't have to be a nightmare, either."

As Fargo recalled Mountain Joe saying earlier, they had not had many run-ins with hostiles, and only ever tangled with a griz once. "Her life with you hasn't been all that bad."

Joe stiffened. "Whose side are you on, damn it? We've been lucky, is all, and no one's luck lasts forever." He clasped his big hands. "Please. I've never begged for anything in all my born days but I'm begging you now. As soon as she is fit to ride, help me throw her over a horse and tie her down. Keep her tied if you have to until you get her to Denver or maybe Saint Louis."

The notion was ridiculous but Fargo did not say so.

"Well? What do you say? Help me do at least one thing right in life. Help me save her from herself."

"I won't take her against her will. She's a grown woman and can do as she pleases," Fargo said.

"You're a powerful disappointment, son," Mountain Joe said, and let out a loud sigh.

The blankets stirred, and Prissy braced her chin in her hand. "Not to me, he's not. Besides, if he carted me off, I'd only come back. You could go as deep into these mountains as you wanted and I would still find you. I swear, Pa, Sometimes you don't have the sense God gave a goose."

"You vex me, girl. You truly do."

"If love is vexing, so be it. I'm sticking with you and that's that, and if you don't like it, you can go beat a tree."

Mountain Joe pushed to his feet so abruptly that he bumped his head on the top of the lean-to. "I think I will before I say something I'll regret." He stomped off, his big hands thrust in his bear coat.

Fargo helped himself to a cup of coffee. As he poured, he commented, "Your father means well."

"I know. He's a kitten at heart but he would never admit it." Prissy slowly sat up and placed a hand to her head.

"How do you feel?"

"Like I have been stomped by Matilda." Prissy smiled and stretched, her bosom swelling against her buckskin dress. She thoughtfully regarded the western horizon. "It will be night soon. Stick around for supper, and after, if you like." Her smile widened. "I'll make it well worth your while."

6

Fargo was no different than most men when it came to women. He had long since given up trying to figure them out. They were as unpredictable as the weather, and seemed to take feminine delight in confusing men no end.

Take Priscilla Howard. She had been hit on the head and rendered unconscious. The blow had left a gash that would take weeks to heal. She had to be in pain. Logic dictated, therefore, that the last thing she would be interested in was the very thing that came to Fargo's mind when she said that she would make his visit well worth his while. To Fargo that had one meaning. As it would to most men. But Priscilla, being female, might not have meant it in the vein Fargo took it. Or so Fargo concluded after half an hour of pondering.

By then Mountain Joe had returned. He had calmed down and was in a surprisingly jovial mood. He agreed heartily when Prissy mentioned she had invited Fargo to stay and, clapping Fargo on the back, earnestly declared, "If she hadn't asked you, I would have. It will be nice to have some company for a change."

That was when Fargo realized all three of them were forgetting something. "What about Captain Preston? He wanted you to eat with him, remember?"

"Until he hands over the bastard who hurt my girl,

him and the rest of his blue bellies can go to hell," Mountain Joe declared.

"You can't blame the captain," Prissy said. "He had nothing to do with it." She pursed her full lips. "Maybe Skye is right. Maybe we should go pay our respects."

A growl of annoyance rumbled deep in Mountain Joe's barrel chest. "First off, I can blame whoever the hell I want. So what if it wasn't Preston who attacked you? It was one of his men and he's responsible for what they do."

"Skye was telling me that they think someone else is lurking about," Prissy remarked.

"And you believe them?" Mountain Joe snorted. "We've been here over two weeks, daughter, and not seen hide nor hair of another living soul." He thrust out his jaw and put his hands on his hips. "Even if they're not to blame, you're in no condition to go traipsing all over creation."

Prissy pointed at the campfires of the troopers. "It's only a short walk, and as I was telling you, I'm fine. My head doesn't hurt much at all."

"We're not going and that's final." Mountain Joe turned to Fargo. "Now are you staying or not?"

"It would be rude to change your mind," Prissy urged.

Fargo grinned. "I wouldn't want that," he said. Was it his imagination, or did her eyes light up with something other than the reflection of the fire?

Joe wanted to cook but Prissy wouldn't let him. She insisted on preparing the meal herself.

For his part, Fargo was content to sip steaming-hot coffee and listen to Mountain Joe chatter on about everything under the sun. At one point Joe mentioned how hard it had been rearing Prissy alone after his wife died, and Prissy piped up with, "You could have remarried, Pa."

47

"What a thing for you to say! Your mother just rolled over in her grave," Mountain Joe chided. He was seated on a short log. "She was my one true love. There can never be another."

"Why, Pa, that was plumb romantic," Prissy said.

"Tease away. But there will come a day when you will meet a man and know he's the one for you. I can't explain it. It just sort of happens. When it does, you're never the same. The two of you become like two halves of a coin, or a knife and a sheath. The one can't live without the other."

Prissy focused on Fargo. "Has anything like that ever happened to you?"

"Not that I know of," Fargo answered. Which was not entirely true. There had been a few women he cared for a great deal. Beyond friendship, beyond merely liking them. In a couple of instances, his feelings bordered on the special relationship Joe had described. But circumstances, and his wanderlust, always compelled him to move on.

A frown curled Prissy's lips. "That's too bad. Maybe one day when you least expect, it will." She had more to say, but footsteps brought the three of them around with their hands streaking to weapons.

"It's only me, folks." Sergeant Hunmeyer halted near the lean-to and doffed his hat.

"What do you want?" Mountain Joe gruffly demanded.

"Begging your pardon, but the captain sends his respects," Hunmeyer said. "He asked me to escort you to his tent."

"We've changed our minds."

"Sir?"

"You heard me, Sergeant. We're staying put. After what happened to my daughter, do you honestly think I would let her anywhere near you boys in blue? You have a bad seed among you, and that's no mistake."

Clearly uncomfortable with the accusation, Hunmeyer protested, "But it might not have been one of us, sir. Our sentries saw—"

Mountain Joe held up a callused hand. "They can claim they saw Satan himself, but I know better. Tell your captain that we mean no slight. I'm only doing what's best for me and mine."

"Very well." Sergeant Hunmeyer stuck his hat back on, nodded at Priscilla, and turned to leave.

"Hold on. I'm not done yet," Mountain Joe said. "Let your captain know that I want all of you gone."

"Sir?"

"Are you hard of hearing? My daughter and I don't care for your company. Strike your camp and leave by noon tomorrow."

Hunmeyer had been making an effort to be polite but now his demeanor changed. "You don't own this valley, mister."

"We were here first."

"That still doesn't give you the right to make demands. Civilians have no authority over the army."

The mountain man reached out and patted his Sharps rifle, which was leaning against a support pole. "This is all the authority I need."

Sergeant Hunmeyer glanced at Fargo as if expecting him to say something, and when Fargo didn't, he said to Mountain Joe, "Are you threatening us? If so, I would advise against it unless you want us to take you into custody and haul you back to Fort Laramie."

"I would like to see you try." Mountain Joe started to rise.

Prissy suddenly stood and put a restraining hand on her father's shoulder. "Enough, Pa. That temper of yours will be the death of you." She bestowed a cold smile on Hunmeyer. "We're not threatening anyone. But we would take it as a kindness if Captain Preston would see fit to honor our request."

"I'll pass on the word, but I wouldn't count on us leaving for two or three days yet." Sergeant Hunmeyer gave a slight bow, did an about-face, and departed.

As soon as he was out of sight, Prissy spun on her father. "I want your word that you won't lift a finger against them."

"Now see here, girl—" Mountain Joe began.

"Your word," Prissy insisted. "Or so help me, I won't speak to you for a month! Make that two months!"

"Calm yourself, child."

That was the wrong thing to say. It only made Prissy madder. "I'm no child. I'm a grown woman. And I know you, Pa. I know how your mind works. So promise me, damn it."

Mountain Joe squirmed like a worm on a hook. He muttered something and glared in the direction of the soldiers. Finally he scowled and sighed and said bitterly, "All right. Have it your way. I promise I won't give them any trouble provided they don't give me cause."

Satisfied, Prissy sank back down. "Good. Now that that's settled, how about we feed our guest before he starves to death?"

Their meal consisted of hot, juicy roasted elk meat cooked in strips, boiled grouse eggs, a salad of clover and chickweed, and a pudding made from wild cranberries mixed with the ground-up inner bark of a pine tree. Prissy also made small cakes.

"I'm sorry we don't have anything fancier," Prissy said as she handed Fargo a tin plate heaped high with food.

"I'm used to living off the land," Fargo assured her. The aroma made his mouth water. Until that moment he had not realized how famished he was. He ate heartily, two helpings of everything, but that was nothing compared to the amount of food Mountain Joe devoured. The man was a bottomless pit. Joe ate at least four pounds of elk meat, occasionally smacking his lips with relish and loudly licking his greasy fingers.

"This is the life! Give me the wide-open spaces any day! I wouldn't trade this for all the gold in creation."

Fargo agreed. To him a cabin or a house or a hotel room was nothing more than a cage. Yet another reason he never stayed in any one place too long.

"We're a lot alike, you and me," Mountain Joe said. "It's too bad you're not in the market for a filly. You'd do for a son-in-law."

"Pa!" Prissy exclaimed.

"Well, it's true," her father said, and sank his teeth into yet another piece of meat, its juice dripping over his chin into his beard.

A vast host of stars sprinkled the firmament when Prissy collected the tin plates and mentioned she was taking them to the stream to wash.

"I'll do it, daughter," Mountain Joe said. "Stay put and rest."

"I can wash a few dishes without help." Prissy strode past him. "A body would think I was stove up, to hear you talk."

Joe gazed at Fargo in mute appeal and jerked a thumb at his daughter. Fargo took that as a hint and fell into step at her side. "Mind if I tag along?"

"Not at all, handsome," Prissy said, and lowered her voice. "To be honest, I was hoping you would." Despite her ordeal she was in remarkably good spirts and practically skipped along.

The stream was about forty feet from the lean-to. The glow of the fire gave way to the dark of night as they went down the bank. Prissy knelt, set the plates down, and raised her arms to the heavens. "Isn't it gorgeous?"

Fargo grunted. The stars were fine but she was finer.

He had a hankering to run his fingers through her lustrous hair.

Prissy patted the ground. "Have a seat. Or are you the shy type?"

"Not that anyone would notice." Fargo curled his legs under him. She was so close that their shoulders brushed, sending a tingle down his arm. He had to restrain himself from embracing her.

"Something the matter?"

"No," Fargo said.

"You're a terrible liar. You act like I have the measles or something. I won't break if you touch me."

"What about that?" Fargo indicated the spot above her left ear where she had been struck.

"What about it?" was her rejoinder. "It stings a little now and then but otherwise it doesn't bother me any." She brought her face near to his. Her warm breath fanned his cheek. "You're as much of a kitten as my pa," she said softly. "But cuddling isn't like riding a horse. I'm not liable to fall off and hurt myself worse."

Fargo chuckled. "Who said anything about cuddling?"

"I did," Prissy said, and pressed her warm lips to his.

A wellspring of carnal craving flowed through Fargo. Wrapping his left arm around her slim waist, he pulled her close. Her mouth parted, permitting him to entwine his tongue with hers. Their kiss lingered a good long while. When they parted, Prissy was breathing heavily.

"That was nice. Real nice. I gather you've had a lot of practice."

"Some," Fargo admitted. He roamed his left hand down her back and cupped her bottom. A low gasp escaped her. He smothered it with another kiss. She looped an arm about him and rested her other hand on his thigh. Twitching below Fargo's belt spurred him into cupping her breast and squeezing. A hiss of pure pleasure showed how much she liked it.

"A gal could make a habit of this" was Prissy's comment when she finally drew back.

"What will your father think?" An image filled Fargo's mind; Mountain Joe, brandishing the Sharps and bellowing that his daughter's virtue had been violated.

"He's not a prude, if that's what you're thinking," Prissy said. "He knows I brought you out here to fool around."

"Lucky me." This time when Fargo kissed her, he shifted so his arms bore her weight and he carefully lowered her onto her back on the soft grass. He stretched out beside her.

A dark halo of luxurious hair framed Prissy's lovely face. She flashed her white teeth encouragingly. Her dress could do little to disguise the twin bulges of her ample breasts. "In case you're wondering, you're not my first."

It puzzled Fargo, her mentioning that out of the blue. Molding his body to hers, he kissed her mouth, her cheeks, her neck, her ears. When he covered both of her melons with his hands, she cooed lustily deep in her throat. He intended to take his time but Prissy had other notions. Her fingers pried at his belt, then at his pants. He nearly gasped when he felt her hand enfold his swollen manhood. Wasting no time, she parted her thighs and drew him between them.

"So soon?" Fargo said.

Prissy's response was to arch her back and impale herself on his pole. In a single swift motion the deed was done. "It's been so long. So very long," she whispered huskily. "Do me. Do me hard."

Fargo obliged.

Later, fully spent, they lay still, Fargo with his head

7

Jarred out of lethargy, Fargo sat up. Prissy had fallen asleep and had not heard the laugh. Rising, he adjusted his pants and his gun belt, and warily crept to the top of the bank. He wished he had the Henry, but he had left it under the lean-to. Palming his Colt, he peered over.

For all of ten seconds Fargo was frozen with shock. He had not known what to expect but he had not expected the grisly spectacle of Mountain Joe thrashing about on the ground with both big hands clasped to his throat in a vain bid to stanch the blood that was spurting in a fine mist.

"Prissy!" Fargo yelled to awaken her, and raced to her father's aid. He reached Mountain Joe just as the mountain man stopped moving. Their eyes met, and in that brief contact Fargo saw Joe's life fade, and something else. He saw undiluted sorrow.

Joe's hands went limp. Dripping scarlet, they slid off his neck, revealing the cause of death; someone had slit his throat from ear to ear. Slit it with such force that Joe had nearly been decapitated.

A shriek nearly shattered Fargo's eardrums. In his daze he had been unaware of Prissy. Her hair disheveled, her buckskin dress askew, she was horror-struck by her father's ghastly end.

"Don't look," Fargo urged, and tried to catch hold

of her, but she would not be denied. She pushed him away.

"Lord in heaven, no!" Sinking to her knees, Prissy cradled her father's head in her lap, heedless of the crimson that stained her dress. "No! No! No! No! No!" she wailed in anguish.

Fargo started to reach for her but thought better of it. He spun on a boot heel, seeking the culprit, but whoever had committed the deed had vanished into the night. His Henry was gone, too. Whoever murdered Mountain Joe had taken it.

The fire was burning low. Fargo quickly added fuel, hoping he might yet glimpse the killer, but although the ring of firelight expanded by twenty feet, it caught no one in its glare.

A commotion had broken out to the north. Figures materialized, rushing toward the clearing. Captain Preston and Sergeant Hunmeyer were the first to arrive, trailed by half a dozen young troopers. To a man, they stopped short and gaped in dismay, even the hardened veteran, Hunmeyer.

Prissy did not notice them. She was bent over her father, weeping in unrestrained grief. Great, racking sobs shook her entire body.

"Who did this?" Captain Preston breathlessly asked.

"You tell me," Fargo said, none too pleasantly.

The implication was not lost on Preston. "All of my men can be accounted for. No one was permitted to leave camp without my say-so."

"Any one of them could have snuck off," Fargo suggested.

"Not with four sentries on duty," Preston disagreed.

"Captain, we should conduct a quick search of the area," Sergeant Hunmeyer proposed. "Before whoever did this can get away."

Preston tore his gaze from the spreading pool of

blood. "Yes. You're right. I should have thought of it myself. Leave two troopers to guard our horses and provisions. Everyone else takes part."

"I'll get right on it." Hunmeyer glanced at Fargo. "Coming?"

Fargo shook his head. Priscilla might need comforting, and after their tryst by the stream the responsibility fell on his shoulders. Not that he minded. For the moment, though, all he could do was wait for the worst of her grief to run its course.

"I take it you didn't see the murder committed?" Captain Preston asked. "You or Miss Howard?"

"No."

"How can that be? Where were the two of you—" Preston caught himself. He glanced at Prissy, then at Fargo. "Oh. I see. I won't pry further. But after all that has happened, I fail to comprehend how you could leave her father alone."

Resentment flared, but Fargo suppressed it. The truth was, the officer had a point. Had they been there, Joe might still be alive. In his defense, Fargo had never imagined the mountain man was in danger. He had assumed the killer was after Prissy, not her father.

"Since there isn't anything I can do for Miss Howard at the moment, I will oversee the search," Captain Preston said.

"Warn your men the killer has my Henry."

"What?" Preston bleated in alarm. "How could you let that happen? Do you realize what it means?"

Yes, Fargo did. The army-issue Starr carbines the troopers were armed with were single-shot weapons. The Henry, on the other hand, sprayed fifteen rounds without having to be reloaded. A tremendous advantage. If the troopers cornered him, the killer could more than hold his own.

Captain Preston smacked his leg in anger. He

glared, then ran off to relay the information to those under him.

Their exchange had gone unnoticed by Prissy. Heedless of the blood, her face was pressed to her father's chest.

Squatting, Fargo draped an arm across her shoulders. He did not say anything. Words were useless at a time like this. He was taken aback when she suddenly flung her arms around his neck and continued to weep in great, racking sobs.

In the meantime, the troopers were spreading out. Preston bellowed orders nonstop. He had them work in pairs, a prudent precaution. Stealth was not in their vocabulary. They stomped and crashed through the underbrush like a herd of agitated buffalo.

The killer, if he was still around, would find it ridiculously easy to avoid them.

By Fargo's reckoning another twenty minutes had gone by when Prissy stopped crying and raised her head. Her eyes were puffy and bloodshot, her cheeks wet, her lips quivering.

"I loved him, Skye. Loved him dearly." Prissy placed her hand on Joe's matted hair. "He may not have been the best father who ever lived, but he always tried to be the best he could be."

There were worse epitaphs, Fargo reflected. "We'll bury him in the morning. I'll dig the grave myself."

"What will I do with him gone? Where will I go?" Prissy was not asking him. She was posing the questions to herself.

Fargo knew the answers as well as she did. She could not stay in the mountains alone. She must head for civilization, whether she wanted to or not.

"This changes everything," Prissy forlornly summed up his thoughts. "My days of being as free as a bird are over."

Fargo had a hunch she would like town life more

than she thought she would. It was a cage, but a gilded cage, with pretty dresses and bonnets and dances on Saturday night and young men come courting. "You'll do fine. You're strong inside, where it counts."

Prissy touched his neck. "Will you go with me? Maybe take me to Denver? It's a mile up in the Rockies, folks say, so I would still be in the mountains."

Fargo hesitated, and she noticed.

"Please. I could just use your company for a bit, if you can spare the time." Prissy sniffled and dabbed at her eyes. "Have you ever been there?"

Fargo had been to Denver many a time. Most of those occasions had been spent in saloons with a bottle of whiskey in one hand and his other wrapped around a voluptuous dove. "Yes."

"Think I'll like it?"

"The locals are a friendly bunch." Fargo went on to tell her that, after the discovery of gold at Cherry Creek nearly three years ago, Denver had become the fastest-growing city west or east of the Mississippi. A stepping-off point for the hordes after the precious yellow ore, Denver was now part of the recently created Colorado Territory. "There are dress shops and social societies for ladies, and carriages to ride around in."

"How would I earn a living? I won't sell my body like so many women do to get by."

"There are plenty of good jobs," Fargo said. "You could work as a seamstress, or in a restaurant." With her looks, she would have no trouble being hired on.

"I'll go there, then," Prissy declared.

It confirmed Fargo's suspicion that the sole reason she had stayed in the wilds was her father. All the while she had secretly pined for the same things most women longed after; a safe place to live, a nice home, a husband to mold to her will, and little ones to bounce on her knee.

"How soon can we leave?"

Fargo told the truth. They would leave tomorrow if it was up to him, but he was obligated to stay with the survey detail until they were done inspecting possible sites.

"How long will that be?" Prissy inquired.

"I'll have to ask Preston," Fargo said. It was his understanding the troopers would head for Fort Laramie in a week or so.

"When we do get to Denver, can you stay with me a spell? Until I get used to all the goings-on?"

Did she have an ulterior motive? Fargo wondered. Such as trying to entice him into staying with her permanently?

As if Prissy had read his thoughts, she said quickly, "Only for a short while." In a tiny voice she added, "I'm all alone now. I don't have anyone else."

That sparked a question. "What about relatives? Don't you have any aunts or uncles or cousins or in-laws?"

"My pa has a sister in Indiana, but he lost touch with her pretty near twenty years ago. She must figure he's long dead." Prissy glanced her father, and her throat bobbed. "Now he really is."

More tears flowed. Fargo patiently waited them out. Now and then he glimpsed the soldiers conducting their search for Joe's slayer. He doubted they would find anyone. But he was mistaken. For presently, to the northeast, there was a shout, and a shot, and someone bawled for help. Troopers converged from all directions, making a tremendous racket. Sergeant Hunmeyer shouted something, and a brief silence ensued. Then Fargo heard the sergeant order everyone back to camp.

Fargo wanted to find out what was going on but he could not leave Prissy there alone. He was going to ask if she would go with him when boots splashed in the stream, and over the bank jogged Captain Preston and Sergeant Hunmeyer, their features grim.

"I came to warn you," Preston said. "One of my men has just been killed. Private Stover. Don't let down your guard for an instant."

"I heard the shot."

"That's not how Private Stover was slain. He and Private Weaver separated to go around a thicket. Weaver heard Stover make a strange sound and found him on his back with a spear through his throat."

"A spear!" Prissy exclaimed. "An Indian killed him!"

Preston nodded. "The other trooper spotted a warrior slinking off and fired a shot, but he doesn't think he hit him."

"The same warrior must have killed my pa."

"Or there might be others," Sergeant Hunmeyer said. "A war party, out for our scalps."

Fargo was skeptical. He had found no trace of Indians anywhere in the vicinity. "Who was the trooper who spotted the warrior?"

"Private Barstow," Captain Preston disclosed. "Another pair, Travis and Koon, thought they caught a glimpse of the savage, too."

Barstow again, Fargo mused. Suspicion flared, but he kept it to himself for the time being.

Sergeant Hunmeyer was scouring the encircling woods. "We can't have our men roaming about in the dark with hostiles lurking about. They'll pick us off one by one."

"I'm pulling my men back," Captain Preston elaborated. "We'll set up a perimeter around our camp and fortify it as best we are able, then wait for daylight. Under the circumstances, it's best if the two of you join us." He motioned. "Out here by yourselves, isolated like this, you're at great risk."

Fargo was inclined to stay where they were but

Prissy answered first. "We'll be glad to. But I can't leave my pa untended. Indians mutilate bodies sometimes."

"I'll send four troopers and have him carried to my tent," Preston offered. He extended a hand. "Come along, Miss Howard."

"We'll wait until your men get here," Prissy said. She stood and went to her father's Sharps. "Don't fret about us. We'll be on the lookout for red devils."

Preston did not like it but he went, Hunmeyer at his heels, saying over his shoulder. "Pack up whatever you want to bring."

Prissy handed Fargo the Sharps. "Keep watch, will you?"

The familiar feel of the heavy rifle brought back memories. Fargo had used a Sharps for years. Reliable and powerful, the large caliber rifle could drop a buffalo from hundreds of yards off. But like the carbines, Sharps were single-shot weapons. In a crisis, a skilled shooter could get off four or five shots in the span of a minute. But that could not begin to compare to the Henry, which could bang off thirty rounds in the same amount of time.

Prissy had emptied the coffeepot and was stuffing it into a pack. "I left our supper plates by the stream," she mentioned.

"We'll get them tomorrow," Fargo said. He placed himself between the woods and her, just in case.

True to Captain Preston's word, a quartet of nervous young troopers presently hastened out of the darkness. One was leading a horse.

"Remember me? Private Weaver?" the tallest introduced himself. "If you don't mind, ma'am, we'll put your pa over this critter and be on our way."

They quickly went about the task, casting repeated glances at the dark wall of vegetation.

Fargo assumed the lead, Prissy at his side. Private

Weaver came next, holding onto the reins. The other three soldiers brought up the rear.

Weaver cleared his throat. "I don't mind telling you, those Injuns have us spooked. Not of us have ever fought redskins before."

Thinking of Barstow, Fargo said, "I doubt you have anything to worry about." No sooner were the words out of his mouth than the night exploded with rapid rifle fire—aimed at them.

8

Fargo reacted instantly. He flung himself at Prissy and bore her to the ground. Twisting as he dropped, he landed on his side and snapped the Sharps to his shoulder. The swift cadence of the shots told him that his own rifle, the missing Henry, was being used against them, with withering effect.

Private Weaver had died with the first shot, his forehead cored completely through. The other troopers spun toward the woods and returned fire. Muzzle flashes were all they had to shoot at. But the shooter was behind a tree while they were out in the open. Like grain falling to a scythe, they were cut down, their torsos peppered.

Even the horse bearing Mountain Joe's body was hit. It whinnied and staggered, then collapsed, pinning its blanket-shrouded burden underneath.

"Pa!" Prissy cried.

Fargo fired at the tree the bushwhacker was behind. It had been so long since he used a Sharps that he had forgotten how much the heavy rifle kicked. He doubted he had hit the killer but he was sure he came close.

The shooting stopped. Receding footsteps pattered, attended by the same maniacal laugh.

Fargo rose as far as his knees. "I need ammunition."

"There's some in my pa's pack, but I left it in the lean-to," Prissy said. She crawled to the dead horse and sought to extricate her father. "Help me, please."

"Stay down," Fargo directed. He was not entirely convinced the killer was gone. It might be a trick to lure them into the Henry's sights.

"Please tell me I'm dreaming, and I'll wake up in a bit and my pa will be alive and everything will be fine."

"Don't fall apart on me," Fargo said. "We'll make it through this if we don't lose our heads." He had seen it happen. People who fell to pieces over the death of a loved one, and lost their own as a consequence.

Shouts heralded the arrival of Sergeant Hunmeyer and eight troopers. Swearing lustily, they examined their dead companions. A few bowed their heads.

Hunmeyer had his men form a circle around Prissy. "We will get you safely to the captain."

"What about my pa?" she said. "We can't just leave him here."

"I will return for the body," the sergeant promised.

One of the young troopers had a query of his own. "Shouldn't we bury our friends before we do anything else?"

"They will still be there in the morning," Hunmeyer said. "The important thing is to protect the living. That includes us."

Additional soldiers had been posted at various points, and were jumping at shadows. A bellow from Hunmeyer snapped them to attention.

Captain Preston was waiting for them.

Fargo had not seen any sign of Private Barstow yet. He glanced from sentry to sentry and finally saw Barstow at the east edge of camp, watching them. Oddly, Barstow was bent forward, his hands on his legs.

The news of the slaughter horrified Captain Preston.

"Four more dead? Dear God. What will I tell the colonel?" He did more of his lip gnawing. "Enough is enough. The savages must not be permitted to strike at us with impunity. Sergeant, I want every man on the perimeter. No one is to fall asleep or I will have them up on charges. Understood?"

"Yes, sir." Hunmeyer hustled his charges to their posts.

Captain Preston turned to Fargo. "I need your best assessment. How many are we up against? Which tribe is it? The Blackfeet? The Bloods? Some other savages?"

"Indians aren't to blame," Fargo said.

"On what do you base this assumption?"

"I heard the killer laugh. Indians whoop. They yell. They shriek. But one thing they do not do is laugh."

"A rather flimsy argument," Captain Preston said. "And not one on which I care to base my decisions."

"Your choice," Fargo responded. His estimation of the officer had fallen a few notches.

"Do you still maintain it is one of my men?"

"Has to be," Fargo said.

Preston scowled and looked at Hunmeyer, who shrugged as if to say he did not believe it was one of their troopers, either. "I'm sorry. Until you can show me a shred of indisputable proof, I can not agree."

Fargo made no attempt to mask his sarcasm. "All I have are bodies." Unless Preston took drastic measures, and soon, there were bound to be more.

Captain Preston turned to his tent and parted the flap. "Here you go, my dear," he said to Prissy. "It's not much, but you will have some privacy."

"I don't know," Prissy said uncertainly. She still had not shaken off the immediate horror of her father's death.

"You should try to rest," Captain Preston urged. "It's the best medicine at a time like this."

"I suppose," Prissy said dully. She was withdrawing into herself. Unless she snapped out of it, by morning she would be barely able to function. She appealed to Fargo. "What do you think?"

"You do need to rest." Fargo handed her the Sharps. "I'll be back in a bit to keep you company."

"Don't be long," Prissy requested. "I don't want to be alone." She went in and pulled the flap shut after her.

Captain Preston shifted toward Fargo. "Now then. About your suspicion—"

"First things first," Fargo said, and wheeling, he ran to where he had left the Ovaro. The pinto was fine. So were the other horses. Additional proof Indians were not anywhere near. Among the Blackfeet, stealing a horse was rated as high a coup as slaying an enemy.

About to return to the tent, Fargo glanced down. He had left his saddlebags draped across his saddle, with the bedroll on top. Now the bedroll was on the saddle and his saddlebags were on top. Someone had rummaged through his belongings. And on the frontier, touching a man's possessions without his permission was cause for slapping leather.

Fargo hunkered and went through his effects. The first saddlebag was as it should be; his spare shirt, an extra red bandana, the needle and thread he rarely used, a bundle of pemmican, and ammunition for the Colt. All were there. But as soon as he opened the second saddlebag, he knew something was missing. The bag did not bulge as it should. Inside were supposed to be a spare pair of buckskin pants, his coffee, his flour, and a box of cartridges for the Henry. He dipped his hand in, and swore.

The Henry ammo was gone.

Fargo slowly uncurled, his mind racing. It was additional proof he was right about the killer being a trooper. An Indian would have taken the ammunition for the Colt, too. He swiveled to the east, seeking sign of Private Barstow, but the straw-mopped soldier was nowhere to be seen.

Fargo bent his steps to the tent. The front flap was tied open. Inside on the cot, her hands clasped on her knees, rocking forlornly back and forth, was Prissy. She would whine pitiably every few seconds, and shudder. Fargo went in. "How are you holding up?"

It was half a minute before Prissy answered. "I'm fine as can be. Can't you tell? So what if my pa is dead? So what if he was the best father who ever lived? So what if I'm all alone in the world?"

Fargo did not like that sound of that. She was losing control. But before he could try to help her, he had a greater problem to deal with. "Where did Preston and Hunmeyer get to?"

"They didn't say."

"Will you be all right by yourself for a few minutes more?"

Prissy uttered a scoffing bark. "Why wouldn't I be? Just because I killed my pa?"

"What are you talking about?"

"I should have been with Pa instead of at the stream with you. My lust killed him, as sure as I'm sitting here."

"That's ridiculous," Fargo said.

"To you, maybe, but not to me." Tears moistened Prissy's eyes, and she sniffled. "I will never forgive myself."

Just then a trooper came running up and bent to peer past Fargo into the tent. "The captain's not here? I need to talk to him right away. Where is he?"

"That's what I'd like to know," Fargo answered. He vaguely recalled that the young man's name was Koon. "Is something wrong?"

"Everything is wrong with this damn detail," Private

Koon declared. "We've been jinxed from the start."
He pivoted and looked wildly about for the officer. "I
just found Bill Travis dead as dead can be."

"Where?"

Private Koon pointed to the southeast, then ran in
the opposite direction. "I think I see Sergeant Hunmeyer!"

To Prissy Fargo said, "Stay put." Then he bounded
to the southeast. It was easy to find the body. Word
had spread and a knot of troopers had already gath-
ered. Fargo shouldered through them, and grimaced.

The killer had a fondness for throats. First he had
thrust a makeshift spear through Private Stover's
throat; then he had slit Mountain Joe's throat from
ear to ear, and now he had slain Private Travis by
burying a knife to the hilt at the base of Travis's
throat.

"He never let out a peep," a trooper commented.

"Those stinking redskins!" growled another.

"How can we fight them when they flit around like
ghosts?" asked a third.

They were near the stream. At that point the bank
on their side was lower than the bank on the other
side. Their side had little vegetation. The other side
had a lot. Fargo stared at the top of the other bank,
worried. "We shouldn't stand out in the open like
this."

"We can't move the body until the captain has seen
it," a trooper told him.

"We would get in trouble."

"Where's Barstow?" Fargo asked. "Wasn't he on
this side of the camp on sentry duty?"

One of the troopers glanced to either side. "I
thought I saw him right before Koon found the body.
I don't know where he got to."

Fargo's uneasiness grew. He was bending to lift
Koon and tote him off, whether they liked it or not,

when Captain Preston, Sergeant Hunmeyer, Private Koon, and two other soldiers arrived.

Preston immediately knelt and needlessly felt for a pulse that was not there, saying in dismay, "Not another one, damn it."

"We shouldn't be in the open like this," Fargo reiterated.

The officer seemed not to hear. "This knife is regulation issue! Koon was murdered by one of our own."

Sergeant Hunmeyer bent for a closer look. "I'll be damned. I owe you an apology, Fargo."

Private Koon bent down, too. His brow knitting, he pointed at the dead man's waist. "It's not Travis's knife, sir. Look. His is still in its sheath."

"That's a break for us," Captain Preston said. "All we have to do is find out whose knife is missing."

"Unless they have a spare," Sergeant Hunmeyer said.

A puzzled expression had come over Private Koon. "See that scrape mark on the end of the hilt, sarge? I think I know who this knife belongs to."

When the trooper did not go on, Captain Preston snapped, "Well? Don't keep us in suspense."

"Sir, I'd be willing to swear on a stack of Bibles that—" Private Koon never finished. Fireflies flamed atop the high bank across the stream, fireflies accompanied by thunder. Lead flew fast and furious. Fargo recognized the blasting of the Henry, and went prone. The others were not as quick.

The first slug smashed into Private Koon's face, dissolving part of a cheek. The second cored the sternum of a trooper to the left of him. Sergeant Hunmeyer started to straighten and was jolted by several slugs in swift succession. In pure reflex Hunmeyer grabbed for his revolver but he was dead before his fingers touched it.

"Get down!" Fargo shouted. Palming his Colt, he

banged two shots at where he believed the killer was hidden, but apparently he missed because the Henry continued to unleash its lethal leaden hail.

Another trooper sprawled forward. A fourth clutched himself and melted in a disjointed heap.

The Henry's one-rifle fusillade ended.

Fargo, Captain Preston, and the two surviving troopers sought cover. From behind a cottonwood Fargo peered into the gloom shrouding the far bank, yearning for a glimpse of the shooter.

Help arrived in the form of the rest of Preston's detail. They were careful not to show themselves.

Captain Preston sidled over to Fargo. "He has us pinned down, but we still have the advantage of numbers."

Fargo reflected that they were down to eight troopers, the captain, and himself. Against a fifteen-shot rifle, it was not an advantage they should rely on.

Preston stared at Hunmeyer. "I've lost my sergeant. The one indispensable member of my command." He clutched at Fargo's arm. "What do you suggest? Should we flank that bank and move in from both sides?"

"You would lose more men."

"If only I had some idea who it is," Captain Preston remarked.

"Seen Private Barstow recently?"

"Who?" Preston gazed about him. "No, as matter of fact, I haven't. Are you suggesting Private Barstow is the killer? That he is the one who stole your rifle?"

"He also took ammunition from my saddlebags, so he has plenty to spare."

Preston stared at the bodies, many of which were contorted in the grotesque convulsions that had seized them as they expired. "I admit Barstow has been a troublemaker. But he's a green recruit from Minnesota. A farm boy, if I remember correctly. He gets

regular letters from home, from his mother, I believe."
Preston shook his head. "No. You must be mistaken.
A boy like that would never do something like this."

At that juncture laughter pealed, and from across
the stream floated a mocking titter. "Are you worried
yet, Captain? You should be."

Preston gripped the cottonwood so hard, his knuckles turned white. "Private Barstow? Is that you?"

"Of course it's me. How stupid are you? Haven't
you figured that out?" Barstow cackled in contempt.

"I don't understand. Why are you doing this? What
do you hope to accomplish?" Preston shouted.

"Don't you get it yet? I'm going to kill every last
one of you sons of bitches."

9

Dumbfounded incredulity silenced Captain Preston. Dazedly, he looked about him like a man who doubted his senses. Some of his young troopers were just as bewildered, but not all.

"I never did like that weasel. He was always griping. Always nitpicking." The speaker was a thick-shouldered private with a square jaw. "He's a shifty cuss through and through."

"None of us much cared for him, Parker," said another soldier. "When he wasn't complaining, he was spewing insults."

Private Parker sighted down his carbine, eager for a target. "It wouldn't surprise me one bit if he was behind the troubles we've been having. The cinches coming loose, the missing watches and razors and money, all of it."

"I never thought of that," said the other man.

"Barstow isn't happy unless he's making others miserable," Private Parker said. "He's bad to the bone, that one."

Fargo had not known that Barstow was held in such low esteem. But then, he spent most every day ranging ahead of the detail, and at night the troopers tended to keep to themselves, which was fine by him since he was a loner by nature.

Captain Preston stirred. "No more talking, men. We

have a crisis on our hands and it must be dealt with."
He drew his revolver, checked that it was loaded. "Private Parker, you are hereby made a sergeant."

"Sir?" the amazed Parker replied, lowering his carbine.

"Under battlefield conditions, and these certainly qualify in my estimation, an officer may promote those under him where necessary," Captain Preston cited regulations. "I have just lost my sergeant. I need a new one. By rights you should rise to corporal before you become a sergeant but I am sure the colonel will sustain my decision."

"Thank you, sir," the brawny Parker said in sincere gratitude. "I'll do the best I can to be worthy of your trust."

"Stay alive, Parker. That's all I ask of you and the rest of these men." Captain Preston rose half a foot or so and regarded the opposite bank. "We must end this, and end it now. On my order we will fan out and rush Barstow."

"No," Fargo said.

All eyes swung toward him, and Captain Preston said a trifle resentfully, "I beg your pardon. I am in command. It is my decision to make."

"He has my Henry, remember?" Fargo reminded him. "And he's proven he's more than a fair marksman. Try rushing him and few of you will reach the other side."

"Do you have a better idea?"

"As a matter of fact, I do. I'll circle around and take him by surprise." Fargo's woodcraft was second to none, and certainly better than that of a Minnesota farm boy. "All you need do is sit tight until it's over."

"But if we lose you—"

"If I'm not back in two hours, get the hell out of here," Fargo directed. "Give my horse and everything

I own to Prissy. She's been all over this country. She can guide you to Fort Laramie as well as I can."

"I'm not sure that is the best recourse," Captain Preston said.

Fargo nodded at the bodies. "Haven't you lost enough men?" The tally stood to climb a lot higher if the officer did not listen to reason.

"Very well," Preston agreed with great reluctance. "I will give you one hour. Not a minute more."

"I need time to work my way around," Fargo said.

"An hour is more than ample. It shouldn't take half that long. He's only on the other side of the stream."

Fargo did not mention that stalking was a slow, painstaking skill, or that Apaches sometimes spent an entire day stalking victims. He simply sank onto his belly and crawled to the right in a wide loop that would bring him to the stream well past the picketed horses. In his right hand he clutched his Colt.

The night was still except for a vagrant breeze that waxed in periodic gusts. In the distance a wolf howled. Closer, wings beat the night air. Fargo breathed in the dank smell of the earth. Soft grass slid under him. He avoided clumps of brush that might rustle and give him away. He could not see the stream but he could hear it. He crawled parallel to the bank until he came to a gap. Removing his hat, he snaked on through.

Flowing water lapped the earth inches from Fargo's nose. He looked to his left. He was about thirty yards from the high bank that concealed Barstow. That should be enough. He eased into the stream. The water was cold on his neck and chest, and he broke out in goose bumps. The level rose slowly, until only his head and his hand with the Colt were above the surface. He hoped there were no deep holes like the one farther down.

Luck favored him. Fargo reached the other side

without being shot at. He crawled part way up the bank and lay shivering. The bout soon passed. Like a turtle poking its head from its shell, he rose on his elbows to see over.

Thick undergrowth fringed the forest. To reach it, he had to cross six feet of open space. For the few seconds that took he would be easy to pick off. He was bucking the tiger. Hopefully, Barstow's attention was on Preston and the troopers.

Fargo would soon find out. He dug his toes into the ground, braced his legs, and launched himself up and over. A tawny blur amid the inky darkness, he gained the undergrowth.

Once again, no shots boomed. No angry shouts were thrown his way. By his reckoning no more than ten minutes had gone by. Everything was going as he wanted it to go.

Fargo now began the stalk in earnest. He did not approach Barstow's hiding place directly but crawled in a half circle that would bring him up on the young killer from the rear. Moving with exquisite slowness, he probed with his fingers for twigs and branches that might crunch or snap under his weight, and silently moved them aside. He skirted a small thicket rather than go through it. The same with a fallen pine. Once, his hand brushed something smooth and scaly. The creature hissed. Fargo tensed, half anticipating the sharp sting of twin fangs laced with venom. He was in rattlesnake country, and rattlers did most of their hunting at night. But the serpent did not strike. Instead, it slithered off and was swallowed by the night.

Fargo let out the breath he had not realized he was holding. He advanced more slowly, wary that the snake might be in the company of others of its kind. But it was the only one he encountered.

In due course Fargo came to the point at which he must turn toward the stream. The seconds seemed like minutes as he inched forward. Trees screened the exact spot. He had to guess how close he was. He was quite near when an unforeseen obstacle presented itself; a large log, directly in his path. He could go around but he had already used up most of the hour Preston had given him.

Fargo went over the log. He avoided scraping his chest and hips and was congratulating himself on how quietly he had done it when his left knee brushed the bark. The sound was not loud but Fargo froze, fearing Barstow had heard. The continued stillness of the woodland reassured him.

Hiking his leg higher, Fargo carefully eased flat. Wriggling on his belly, he slid in among a last belt of trees. He heard nothing out of the ordinary. He detected no movement.

Only a strip of brush and a lone tree now separated Fargo from the high bank. He slid past the brush and stopped behind a pine. With a sinking feeling in his gut, he threw himself forward and aimed at the spot where Private Barstow should be.

Only Barstow wasn't there.

Fargo's blood became ice. While he had been stalking Barstow, Barstow had been stalking what was left of the detail. *The troopers!* He scrambled up the bank to warn them. By now Barstow must be close enough to spray them with slugs. He came to the top and rose onto his knees. Waving an arm to attract their attention, he hollered, "Watch yourselves! Barstow isn't here!"

Captain Preston stepped into view and put a hand to his mouth. "What was that, you say? He got away?"

"Watch out for Barstow!" Fargo bellowed. To his dismay, he saw several troopers move toward the stream. They did not seem to understand.

"We haven't seen him!" Captain Preston shouted.

The new sergeant, Parker, and the rest were foolishly showing themselves, only a few with their carbines at the ready.

"No!" Fargo cried. "Take cover!"

Then it happened. That which Fargo was trying to warn them against. Mantled in shadow, a figure reared behind them. The Henry's brass receiver glinted dully as it was trained on the unsuspecting troopers.

Fargo rose higher. "Behind you!" he roared. He tried to aim but one of the soldiers blundered into his sights. "Barstow is behind you, damn it!"

At last Captain Preston comprehended. He whirled, or started to. A slug from the Henry caught him squarely between the shoulder blades and ruptured the front of his chest.

The Henry cracked in steady cadence as Barstow methodically worked the lever, gunning down target after target. Caught flat-footed, the troopers were slow to react. Four had joined Preston in oblivion when Parker and another man finally got off shots of their own. In the blink of an eye, the wily Barstow seemed to vanish into thin air.

The few troopers left turned in all directions in confusion. "Where did he get to?" one marveled.

Fargo hurtled down the bank and into the stream. His legs churning, splashing mightily, he came to the other side.

Parker heard him, and turned. "The captain is dead," he stated the obvious. "What do we do?"

"Hug the ground!" Suiting his own action to his suggestion, Fargo flattened. As happenstance would have it, he was next to Preston. The dead officer's wide eyes were fixed on the heavens. Under him a pool of blood was spreading.

"Do we stay here or hunt for him?" Parker had the presence of mind to whisper. "I've never done anything like this before. I need your help."

"We do neither," Fargo said. "We get Prissy Howard and light a shuck."

"But what about Barstow? We can't just ride off. He has a lot to answer for." Parker bobbed his chin at his fallen friends.

"The army will send someone to deal with him," Fargo explained. "We'll leave him afoot by taking all the horses."

It took a few seconds for Parker to grasp the consequences. A slow grin spread across his face. "He won't get far on foot. With any luck, the hostiles will find him and skin him alive."

"We can always hope," Fargo said.

Parker whispered orders and the five of them slowly worked their way toward the tent, Fargo in the lead. He regarded every shadow as a potential threat, every sound, however slight, as possibly made by the killer. They neared a back corner of the tent. Fargo was the first to note that it leaned slightly, as if bending to a strong wind. But there was no wind. Caution forgotten, thinking only of Prissy, he shoved off the ground and raced to the front.

The flap still hung open. It revealed that the front support pole was cracked, the cot overturned. Preston's personal effects had been scattered about.

Otherwise, the tent was empty.

"He's taken Miss Howard!" Parker cried in horror. "We have to find them! There's no telling what he'll do to her."

Laughter rose out of the forest, seeming to come from different directions at once.

Fargo and the troopers whirled and crouched but there was no one to shoot.

"I would hold my fire were I you." Barstow tittered like it was all a giant game to him. "If you don't, you have only yourselves to blame for what I do to this pretty peach of a gal."

"I want to kill him so bad," Parker said so that only Fargo heard.

He was not the only one, Fargo mused. All he asked was a clear shot. One clear shot.

"I can see you but you can't see me," Barstow crowed. "I could pick you off if I wanted. But that would end the fun too soon."

Parker raised his voice. "Let us take Miss Howard and go. I promise to leave you a horse and grub. You'll be free to do whatever you want. We won't come after you. Just don't hurt her."

"You're as stupid as Preston," Barstow responded. "You still have no idea how little any of your lives mean to me."

"I do," Fargo let him know. He hoped to keep the cold-blooded monster talking so he could pinpoint exactly where Barstow and Prissy were.

"Is that you, scout?" Barstow snickered. "What is it they call you? Oh, yes. I remember now. The Trailsman. The famous frontiersman. But you're not so special. I've outwitted you at every turn."

Fargo simmered inside. There was no denying that, so far, things had gone entirely Barstow's way.

"Cat got your tongue?" Barstow taunted.

Fargo refused to answer.

"Or is it you're afraid for the woman? I saw the two of you together, you know. It was quite entertaining."

By now Fargo had a fair idea of where the killer was. But he could not see him. He consider working his way around.

"Her father dozed off waiting for the two of you to come back. It was simple to slit his throat."

"What do you want from us, Barstow?" Parker shouted. "Can't we talk this out?"

More cold laughter rent the dark. "Jackasses. Every last one of you. I should think by now it would be as plain as plain can be. The only thing I want from each and every one of you is for you to die."

"Why?" Parker cried. "What have we ever done to deserve this?"

Barstow's next laugh was the most maniacal yet. "Deserve has nothing to do with it. I kill because I like to. Get ready. You too, Fargo. Dying time is here."

10

"He's loco," a trooper breathed. "Plumb mean loco."

"Hush up," Parker said. "Do you want him to hear you? Rile him, and there's no telling what he'll do to Miss Howard."

Fargo's eyes bored into the gloom. He was hoping Barstow would show himself, if only for a fraction of an instant. That was all it would take to snap off a shot and end the nightmare.

Silence fell except for the nervous shifting of the young soldiers. Several minutes went by. The breeze picked up, stirring the trees.

Parker fidgeted and glanced at Fargo. "Why doesn't he say something? What is he up to?"

Fargo was wondering the same thing. "Barstow?" he hollered. He thought of Prissy, and what Barstow might be doing to her.

There was no answer.

"I don't like this," a trooper said. "I don't like this one bit."

Neither did Fargo. He came to a decision. "Get to the horses and get the hell out of here. Take mine with you."

"What about you?" Parker asked.

"Miss Howard is out there somewhere. I aim to find her." Fargo started to rise but Parker caught hold of his sleeve.

"Hold on. You do that and he's liable to kill her."

"He plans to kill her anyway, no matter what we do," Fargo enlightened him. Barstow might be murdering Prissy right that moment.

"Then what good would it do for us to leave?"

"You get to live." Thinking that was sufficient, Fargo again went to move off but Parker did not let go.

"So you're saying you want us to turn tail? I can't speak for the rest but I'm no coward, Mr. Fargo. I want to help."

"Me too," said another. "That bastard has killed our friends. If we run off, I'd never be able to look myself in the mirror."

A third trooper nodded his agreement. The fourth swallowed hard; then he nodded, too.

Fargo reflected a moment. "All right. But we do this my way? Agreed?"

"No argument there," Parker said. "I'm new at this sergeant business. And folks say you've done more than your share of fighting Injuns and such."

Through Fargo's mind flicked the faces of some of the renegades, outlaws, cutthroats, and hostile Indians whose lives he had ended one way or another. In every single instance it had been a case of kill or be killed. He never sought out trouble; trouble always sought him. It came from living on the frontier, of roaming untamed territory haunted by two-legged wolves who regarded everyone else as sheep and thought they had the right to prey on those sheep as they pleased. He invariably proved them wrong.

"Mr. Fargo?" Parker said.

Fargo motioned for them to come closer. "The first thing is to make sure Barstow can't escape." He wagged his Colt at a stocky soldier and the one who had swallowed hard. "Take the horses and head for the pass. Wait there until daylight. Then one of you ride back to the ridge above the stream. Fire three shots. If you hear three in return, it's safe to come down. If you don't, head for Fort Laramie." He paused. "Any question?"

"Just one," the stocky soldier said. "Which direction is west? Without a compass I can't rightly tell."

The other trooper Fargo had picked nodded. "I would know if the sun was up. But stars don't rise in the east and set in the west like the sun does."

"Maybe we should stick togther," Parker suggested. "I can just see them wandering around lost as hell."

So could Fargo. "Forget the pass. The two of you go over by the horses and hide. If Barstow tries to ride off, shoot him in the back."

"In the back?" The stocky soldier was stunned.

"You can ask him to turn around and give him the chance to shoot you," Fargo said. "But he's awful quick with that rifle." *His* rifle, which he was determined to get back. "Off you go," he shooed them. "Remember to keep low."

The pair jogged off.

"What about Tom and me?" Parker whispered. He was not as nervous as the rest, which said a lot about his character. Captain Preston had done right in choosing him to replace Hunmeyer.

"Stay close to me but not too close. One to my right, one to my left. When I stop, both of you stop. If Barstow shoots at us, look for the muzzle flashes and keep firing until I say to stop."

"What if you're killed?"

"Fall back with your friends and hide near the horses. Sooner or later Barstow will make a try for them." Fargo looked at each young face in turn. "Ready?"

"Lead the way," Parker said eagerly. "We have us a rabid dog to dispose of."

Fargo admired their grit. He tended to forget that while most army recruits were young and green as grass, they had proved their mettle time and again when courage and devotion to duty were called for. Hardihood ran in their veins. Less than a hundred years ago, their forefathers had fought for independence. Ever since, in war after war, they always came through.

"Remember. Stay close." Fargo padded into the trees. He made scarcely any sound. The two troopers were not as quiet but they were doing their best.

The wind grew stronger. It complicated things. The rustle of limbs and leaves and the sway of vegetation would mask Barstow's movements.

Fargo strained his senses to their utmost. He roved to the west, then to the north. The two troopers mimicked his every movement. But they found nothing. Fargo swung east. When he came to the stream he bore to the south and presently was back where they had begun, near the tent. The better part of an hour had been spent in the search. "Damn," Fargo vented his spleen.

"Where can that devil have gotten to?" Parker asked in exasperation. "He has to be around here somewhere."

"Maybe the others have seen him," Tom said.

Fargo doubted it or they would have heard gunfire. But he glided toward the horse string anyway. The animals stood with their ears pricked and their nostrils flaring. Several pranced in agitation.

The other two troopers did not come out of hiding to greet them.

Parker was turning every which way. "That's strange. Where did Charlie and Dodson get to? They were supposed to be watching the animals."

Fargo crept along the row of horses. He raised his

leg to step over what he took to be a downed tree limb, then realized the truth; it was a carbine. Scooping it up, he held it for the others to see.

"Oh, hell," Parker said.

"He's killed them, hasn't he?" The whites of Tom's eyes were showing. "He'll kill us next if we're not careful."

"Don't panic," Fargo said. He went a little farther, and stopped cold. He had almost stepped on the stocky soldier. Pallid flesh lent the corpse a ghostly aspect. Like Mountain Joe, the young man's throat had been slit. But that was not all. Both his eyes had been gouged out and his nose chopped off. The eyeballs had then been placed on his chest, eyes up, with the piece of nose between them.

"I'm going to be sick!" Tom declared and, turning away, fulfilled his own prediction.

Parker blanched but had a stronger stomach. "We're not fighting a human being," he said softly. "We're fighting a demon."

Fargo was unaffected. He had seen worse. The mutilation of enemies was a common practice among some Indian tribes, and there was no shortage of renegade whites who took sadistic delight in whittling on people as they would on wood. "Keep your eyes peeled," he warned. "Barstow can't have gone far." The fresh blood oozing from the stocky soldier's eyes was proof of that.

They waited for Tom to recover, then moved on. A pair of odd marks gave Fargo pause. Something had been dragged across the ground. Something, or someone. He parted waist-high weeds.

It was Dodson.

Tom was sick again, in great racking heaves. Parker, too, doubled over, but all he did was turn a greenish shade.

"If you want, stay here," Fargo whispered. "I'll go on alone."

"Nothing doing." Parker had more sand than many men twice his age. Hefting his carbine, he declared, "Where you go, I go."

Tom followed, as well, but Fargo had the impression that, given his druthers, Tom would rather be anywhere on the planet than where they were. He was deeply afraid, and he could not hide it.

Fargo seldom gave in to fear. He had survived too many perilous scrapes, seen too many atrocities. To the young troopers this was the most horrific night of their lives. To him it was as ordinary as dishwater.

"Hey!" Tom forgot himself and yelled. He was looking over his shoulder. "Am I mistaken, or is one of our horses missing?"

Fargo had been focused on the woods. He had not noticed the gap in the string. It could only mean one thing. Barstow had taken a mount and was long gone. Fargo lowered his Colt. "The worst is over." But he could not have been more wrong.

A whinny snapped Fargo around. His piercing lake blue eyes narrowed, and then widened.

Prissy was on the missing horse, a gag in her mouth, her wrists bound behind her, a noose around her throat. The other end of the rope had been tied to a tree.

Fargo took several swift strides but stopped when the demon, as Parker called him, materialized as if out of thin air, pointing the Henry at Prissy's head. "That's far enough, scout."

Prissy was weeping. Her cheeks and chin glistened but she did not utter a sound. Her eyes held mute appeal.

"Be so good as to drop your guns," Barstow directed.

"Like hell," Parker said.

Barstow laughed. "Need I point out what will happen if you don't? One swat to this horse, and your precious Miss Howard will swing by the neck until she is dead, dead, dead." He cackled with glee at the prospect.

Parker took a heated step. "You're scum, Leroy. As low as a person can get. Threatening a girl who can't do you any harm."

"Male, female, it makes no difference to me," Barstow said diffidently. "They all die the same." He brought his free hand close to the horse. "Why haven't you dropped those guns yet? Surely you don't think I'm bluffing?"

Fargo refused to endanger Prissy more than she already was. He set the Colt on the ground and elevated his arms.

"There. That wasn't so hard, was it? Now it's your turn, Parker, and then Tom Delaney."

"I won't," Tom said.

Parker reached for his fellow trooper's carbine. "Yes, you will. We took an oath to protect lives, remember?"

Tom still balked. "I don't care. As soon as we put our guns down, he'll kill us. I know he will. And I don't want to die."

"We have to," Parker insisted, and placed his own carbine at his feet as an example. "Your turn."

"No!" Wheeling, Tom Delaney bolted, but he only managed a few strides before the Henry banged and the middle of Delaney's head burst like overripe fruit.

Parker instantly bent toward his carbine.

"Ah, ah, ah," Barstow said, training the Henry on him. "Touch it and you shorten the little time you have left."

Parker was past caring. "Go ahead! Finish it! I'm the last one."

"You're forgetting our scout," Barstow responded. "I'd like for both of you to take part in what comes next. It's more fun when there's an audience."

"You wouldn't," Parker said.

"Of course I would." Barstow turned to do the deed. "This should be interesting. I've never hanged anyone before."

Fargo had been biding his time, praying Leroy Barstow would make a mistake and give him the opening he needed. But time had run out. If he was to save Prissy, he must act, and act now. Accordingly, he hurled himself at Barstow. Out of the corner of his eye he glimpsed young Parker doing the same. They were close enough that one of them just might reach the maniac.

The Henry boomed twice, the second time practically in Fargo's face. He felt a tremendous blow to his forehead, and his legs swept out from under him. The flash and the smoke blinded him. He heard thrashing sounds, and a flailing arm hit his shoulder. Blinking to clear his vision, he saw Parker, prone and lifeless.

"Idiots," Barstow said.

Fargo tried to rise but a wave of nausea and dizziness overcame him and he sank back.

"Are you ready, gal?"

Pinpoints of light danced before Fargo's eyes. There was a whoop, and a loud smack, then the drum of hooves. Suddenly he could see Prissy, kicking at the end of the rope, her body a bow. "No!" he raged, and made it to his elbows before another blow to his head left him teetering on the brink of consciousness.

Strident laughter pealed. A hand roughly grabbed the front of Fargo's shirt. "Take a good look, scout! She doesn't have long left."

As if through a long tunnel, Fargo saw Prissy convulsing. A few final kicks, and her body went limp. The tunnel became the muzzle of the Henry, inches from his eyes. The world faded in and out but he could still hear.

"And so it ends. I must say, after all the tales I've heard, you were a powerful disappointment."

There was more but Fargo was sinking into a bottomless well. He caught only snatches: "too easy," "want you to suffer," "beat the great scout." Then the blackness claimed him, and there was nothing, absolutely nothing at all.

11

Fort Laramie had a long history. It began as a trading post back in 1834. It was called Fort William for a while, after William Sublette, an early figure in the fur trade. Then it was called Fort John. Finally it occurred to someone to name it after the river it was near, and the post became known as Fort Laramie. The river itself was named after a Frenchman, Jacques Laramie, who had the misfortune to run into a band of unfriendly Arapahos while setting a trapline.

The post was intended to protect wagon trains bound for Oregon country, as well as those who decided the Laramie River region had just as much to offer, and stayed. Two companies of mounted riflemen and one company of infantry had the unenviable task. Unenviable, because most of the neighboring tribes resented the white invasion in general and the presence of the fort in particular.

Colonel Crane was the officer who had sent out the survey detail. Tall and slim, he always wore pressed uniforms and boots polished to a sheen. His office reflected his belief that neatness and efficiency went hand in hand.

Fargo had scouted for Crane in the past, and played cards with him a few times. They were not the best of friends but they got along tolerably well. At the moment, though, Colonel Crane was distinctly unhappy.

"You're asking a lot. My superiors would not approve."

Fargo was straddling a chair catty-corner to the colonel's immaculate desk. Since Prissy's death, a scowl had become a permanent fixture on his face, and now that scowl deepened. "Whether I shoot him or he hangs doesn't matter, just so long as he pays."

"I agree Barstow deserves to be put to death," Colonel Crane said in the clipped manner he had.

"Then let me go after him."

Crane leaned back and made a teepee of his fingers. "I'll be frank with you. I'm concerned that you are more interested in revenge than justice." He held up a slender hand when Fargo went to interrupt. "Let me finish. After what you went through, you have every right to want to kill him. But the army abides by regulations, and those regulations state that I must have him duly taken into custody and brought back here to face a court-martial."

"I can do that," Fargo said.

"Were it only up to me, I would let you. But regulations require it be done by a member of the United States Army." Again Crane held up his hand. "I know what you are about to say. You have been a scout in our employ. But you have never worn a uniform. You have never actually enlisted."

Fargo's temper was fraying. They had hashed this over several times during the two weeks he had been recovering. "Damn it, Alex. He wiped out the entire detail. He murdered two civilians, one of them a woman." For a moment Fargo was back in the mountains, the blackness closing in, Prissy bucking in her final agonies. It was like having a knife twisting in his gut.

"I still can't quite believe it. A new recruit, killing all those men. Preston and I were good friends, and Sergeant Hunmeyer was as professional as they come.

How they let Barstow get the better of them, I will never understand."

"Barstow is a natural-born killer," Fargo said.

"Perhaps you are right. I've made a few inquiries. Apparently Leroy Barstow has a history of violence."

"Tell me more." Fargo had learned long ago that when tracking an animal, or a man, it helped to know their habits.

"Personnel files are confidential. But if anyone has the right to know, you do." Colonel Crane leaned forward. "Barstow was raised on a small farm in southern Minnesota, near a settlement called Jaflyn. He enlisted a year ago, shortly after he turned eighteen."

"Hardly the makings of a killer," Fargo remarked.

"Not at first glance. But what none of us knew was that Barstow did not enlist because he wanted to. He enlisted because he had to."

"Had to?"

"It seems he got into trouble with the law. Something to do with a young woman. Her parents wanted him put behind bars but she begged the court to go easy on him, so the judge gave him a choice."

"Prison or the army," Fargo said in mild disgust. It was not the first time a judge had done that. Some judges were of the opinion the military could turn wayward young lawbreakers into law-abiding citizens.

"Precisely. Barstow naturally chose the army. But the judge had misgivings. Barstow had been in trouble before. Once for killing a neighbor's cow that strayed onto the Barstow farm. Another time for knifing a rival over the affections of the young woman who begged he be spared."

"He wasn't put on trial?"

"No. He was only thirteen, and the other boy was not badly hurt. So Barstow was given a slap on the wrist and released."

The information was interesting but did not account for why the son of a farmer had turned into a cold-blooded killer. Fargo mentioned as much.

"That's where I can't help you. I don't have enough information. But if you still want to go after him, I'll give my consent."

Fargo came out of his chair, smiling for the first time since Barstow had nearly caved in his skull with the Henry. "I'm obliged."

"You didn't let me finish." Colonel Crane folded his arms across his chest. "I will give my consent, yes. On one condition."

Hiding his annoyance, Fargo said, "Let me hear it."

"Better yet, I will let you meet it." Colonel Crane stood and went to the door. "You may come in."

A stout-legged slab of muscle in a sergeant major's uniform entered and came straight to the desk. A sergeant major was the highest rank an enlisted man could attain, short of becoming an officer, and those who wore the chevrons were considered the best the army had to offer. The sergeant major stayed at attention even after Colonel Crane sat down.

"You may sit, Sergeant Macon."

"Thank you, sir."

The name pricked at Fargo's memory. A few years ago, in the middle of the summer, a patrol had been cornered in a box canyon by a Cheyenne war party. All their horses but one had been killed, and they were down to a pitiful few handfuls of food and hardly any water. In the dead of night their sergeant climbed on the last horse, fought his way out of the canyon, and brought reinforcements. His heroism made the newspapers. The name of that sergeant had been James Macon.

Colonel Crane introduced them. With a twinkle in his brown eyes, he said, "As you have no doubt guessed, Sergeant Macon is the condition I alluded to."

"You want me to take him along?" Fargo resented the notion that he needed a nursemaid.

"Quite the contrary," Colonel Crane said. "I want *him* to take *you* along. Sergeant Macon has been assigned to find Private Barstow and return him to Fort Laramie. At his discretion you may go with him to Minnesota. But understand something." Crane's tone lost some of its warmth. "The sergeant is in charge. You are to treat his wishes as if they were mine. Under no circumstances, none whatsoever, is Private Barstow to be harmed. The army desires to make an example of him, and we can not do it if he is dead. If you agree to these terms, then the two of you can leave first thing in the morning."

Fargo waged an internal war with himself. His pride against his thirst for vengeance. He almost stormed out. He would find Barstow on his own and spare the army the time and expense of the court-martial.

"What will it be?"

"I hope the sergeant doesn't snore," Fargo said.

Not only did the sergeant seldom snore, he did not talk a lot, either. Macon was taciturn by nature, so much so that Fargo often had to draw him out to glean information. Fargo learned that the sergeant major had been born in New Jersey but came west at the tender age of four with his parents and siblings. Macon lied about his age to enlist early, and the army had been his whole life ever since.

"There's nothing I love more than wearing this uniform," Macon said one evening as they sat around the campfire sipping coffee.

"Do you like the excitement?" Fargo asked. He knew some soldiers who thrived on skirmishes with hostiles.

"Or is it you have a strong sense of duty?" Other soldiers served out of a devotion to their country.

Macon surprised him by answering, "Neither. I like army life because it is the most orderly life anywhere."

This was a new one on Fargo, and he said so.

"Army life is about discipline, about following regulations, about doing things a certain way."

"And you actually like that?" One of the reasons Fargo had never enlisted was that he could not bear the notion of having every aspect of his life dictated by the very regulations Macon touted. A soldier's daily routine was always the same; up at reveille, a quick breakfast, fall out on the parade ground, drill and work and work and drill until supper, then maybe an hour or two to relax in the barracks before lights-out. Fargo would be bored silly in two days.

"It fits me," Sergeant Macon said. "I'm orderly in my personal habits, so I have no problem adjusting."

They had been on the trail to Minnesota for over a week, and Fargo had yet to bring up the subject he most wanted to talk about. He did so now. "About Leroy Barstow—"

Sergeant Macon did not let him finish. "I am under orders to bring him back alive, and I always carry out my orders."

"Always?" Fargo repeated.

"Without fail." Macon was not bragging. He was stating a fact.

"You've read my report," Fargo said. "You know what he did. You know how many of your fellow troopers he killed. To say nothing of hanging an innocent young woman."

"I am familiar with the details," Sergeant Macon said. "It is too bad about Hunmeyer. He and I were close friends."

"Doesn't it make you mad? Don't you want to get back at Barstow?" Fargo asked.

"My personal feelings do not enter into it. I do what the army wants me to do, not what I want to do."

"No man is an anvil," Fargo said.

Macon's lips quirked in a grin. "Maybe not. But that's how I am, and that's how it will be. We are going to bring Barstow back to Fort Laramie alive and in one piece, whether you want to or not."

"He won't come willingly."

"No doubt," Macon said. "But we are still required to take him alive. It might be difficult but nothing is impossible. He's only a farm boy, after all."

"He might force you to kill him. What then? What if Barstow leaves you no choice?"

Macon was thoughtful a bit. "I will cross that bridge when I come to it. In the meantime, keep in mind what I have told you. If you try to go against the army's wishes, I will take whatever steps are necessary to stop you."

"In other words," Fargo translated, "you would shoot me to save him."

"Only if you force me to."

"Thanks for telling me," Fargo said dryly.

"It is not personal," Macon sought to assure him. "I am only doing my duty. For me, duty comes before all else."

"I understand."

"But you are not happy with my decision." Macon made it a statement, not a question.

"You weren't there," Fargo said. "I made the same mistake you're making. I thought of him as a farm boy and nothing more. But Barstow likes to spill blood. He is snake mean, with no regard for anyone but himself. He snuffs out lives like you would snuff out a candle. He enjoys it. Enjoys seeing things suffer and squirm."

"You make him sound like the devil incarnate."

"If he's not, he's damn close to it," Fargo said. "A trooper by the name of Parker called Barstow a demon, and it fits."

Macon chuckled. "Why is it scouts exaggerate so much? I've never met one yet who can stick to the facts and only the facts. Scouts have to turn everything into a tall tale."

"You think that now," Fargo said. "You won't by the time this is over. You have no idea what you are up against."

"Surely you are not suggesting I am not equal to the task?" Macon sounded slightly piqued.

"All I'm saying is that Leroy Barstow is one of the most dangerous men I have ever run across, and I've tangled with everything from Apaches to outlaws with bounties on their heads." Fargo rested his forearms on his knees. "Don't treat Barstow as you would most other men. When you take him into custody, *if* you do, throw manacles on him and keep them on until you reach the fort."

"I intend doing just that," Macon said. "I appreciate your concern. I truly do. But I anticipate few difficulties. Not when there are two of us."

"There were ten times that many in the detail he wiped out." Fargo had said all he was going to say. He had tried to warn the sergeant major and been rebuffed. Whatever befell Macon was on Macon's shoulders, not his. "As for me, I gave my word to Colonel Crane. I won't shoot Barstow the minute I see him."

"Then we are in agreement." Sergeant Macon refilled his tin cup and sat back. Twice he looked at Fargo as if he had something on his mind. Finally he got it out. "About your report. Barstow really hung that poor woman? Right in front of your eyes? And then did those terrible things to her body?"

All Fargo did was grunt. He did not care to be reminded.

"He certainly has a lot to answer for, and I am

confident he will," Sergeant Macon declared. "You'll see. He's as good as caught."

Fargo knew better. They would be lucky to leave Minnesota alive.

12

From a distance Jaflyn was a drab collection of log and plank buildings clustered like so many squat tombstones. In the heat of a summer's day the settlement was as unremarkable as sweat.

Southern Minnesota had a reputation as a farmer's paradise. Mile after mile of gently rolling terrain, with some of the richest soil anywhere. Water was plentiful and game was abundant.

Two aspects of the region, however, were not to everyone's liking. The first was Minnesota's winters. They were bitterly cold. It was not unusual for the thermometer to plummet in December and not rise again until April or May. Heavy snowfalls were frequent.

The other drawback had nothing to do with the climate and everything to do with keeping one's hair. It was the Sioux. The tribe resented the white intrusion. Although an uneasy truce had existed for a few years, it was not uncommon for lone travelers and families at isolated homesteads to disappear. Resentment had grown on both sides to the point where there was talk that the Sioux might go on the warpath.

Fargo had been to Minnesota several times. He had endured the fierce winters and fought hostile Sioux. He had visited settlements as small as Jaflyn and thought he knew what to expect: friendly folks who greeted strangers with a warm smile and a strong handshake, their community a bustling beehive of activity, their buildings clean and well maintained.

Jaflyn was different. The only sign of life as Fargo and Sergeant Macon rode in was a big gray mongrel dozing under the overhang of the feed and grain. It bared its fangs and growled.

The single dirt street was empty of not only people, but horses as well. That struck Fargo as downright unnatural. There were *always* horses. Yet there the hitch rails stood, serving no purpose other than to gather dust.

In addition to the feed and grain there was a general store, a millinery, a stable, and houses and cabins. A fine sheen of dust covered every one. Even the windows had a film of dust. It lent the impression that the settlement had been abandoned and long neglected, but Fargo glimpsed pale faces at several of the dusty windows, faces that quickly retreated into shadow.

Much to Fargo's regret, notable by its absence was any semblance of a saloon. Fargo could guess why. Jaflyn's God-fearing citizens did not permit anything that smacked of evil. To them, liquor and cards and women in too-tight dresses were Satan's way of luring the foolhardy into eternal perdition.

Fargo licked his dry lips and wished Jaflyn was in Kansas. At least there the God-fearing permitted themselves a few vices.

Sergeant Macon broke another of his long silences. "Where is everyone?"

"If we were in Mexico I would say it was siesta," Fargo remarked. He reined the Ovaro to the rail in front of the general store. "Maybe some Sioux have been seen in the area and everyone is staying inside." It was the only explanation he could think of.

"Do you suppose it's smallpox or the plague?" Mason wondered.

Fargo had not thought of that. Sickness could account for the absence of people. His skin crawled at the thought that a quarantine might be in effect. But he saw no signs to that effect. "Let's go in and ask."

A tiny bell tinkled as Fargo pushed the door open with his toe. He entered, his right hand close to his Colt. Spurs jangling, he walked down an aisle of untidy shelves to a counter. Behind it was a dark doorway.

"How peculiar," Sergeant Macon said. "Maybe the owner is in the back taking a nap."

Fargo thumped the counter with his fist. "Anyone here?" he shouted.

Several seconds went by. Then from out of the dark doorway came strange sounds. A thump, followed by the scrape of what might be a shoe or a boot. They were repeated, *thump, scrape, thump, scrape,* louder each time.

"Who's back there?" Fargo demanded. "Show yourself."

"What do you think I'm doing? Hold your britches on." A figure materialized, a stoop-shouldered apparition with gray hair and a speckled chin. He had a cane in one hand, and dragged his left leg after him. "I'm coming as fast as I can."

"We're in no hurry," Sergeant Macon said.

The proprietor came to the counter and stood sucking air into his lungs, as if walking had exhausted him.

Macon proved to be the most polite sergeant in the army. "Are you all right? We can come back later if now is inconvenient."

"No, no. I'm just not as spry as I used to be." The man held out a spindly hand. "I'm Ira Spivey, by the way."

Shaking Spivey's hand was like shaking dry bones. Fargo introduced himself and the sergeant. "We're hoping you can help us."

"Be glad to if I can," Spivey said. "We don't often get strangers. Are you on your way to Mankato?"

"We're looking for someone," Fargo said.

The sergeant picked that moment to interrupt. "What happened to your leg and shoulder, if you don't mind my asking?"

"Not at all." Spivey gave his left leg a smack with his cane. "I took a bad fall a few years ago. Lost all the feeling from the knee down."

The bell tinkled. Into the store came a middle-aged woman in a homespun dress, her hair done up in a bun. Her expression was downcast. She was staring at the floor and did not notice Fargo or Macon until she was almost on top of them. Then she gave a start, her right hand rising to her throat. "Oh! Forgive me. I nearly walked into you."

Her left arm, Fargo saw, appeared to be crippled. She held it close to her bosom, her wrist bent in a way wrists were not made to bend.

Sergeant Macon removed his hat. "That's quite all right, ma'am. It's we who should apologize for giving you a scare."

"This is Mrs. Gotz," Spivey said. "She and her husband have a farm a few miles south of Jaflyn."

"How do you do," Mrs. Gotz said with a nervous smile. She caught Fargo staring at her arm and self-consciously covered it with her good arm, saying softly, "I got this when I was kicked by a horse."

Macon shot Fargo a glance that suggested he wanted to kick him in the shins. "We're sorry to hear that, ma'am. I'm sure my friend meant no disrespect. He's a scout, and you know how scouts can be."

"What the hell is that supposed to mean?" Fargo snapped.

Sergeant Macon smiled warmly at Mrs. Gotz. "Maybe you or Mr. Spivey would be so kind as to direct us to the Barstow farm."

The store owner visibly stiffened.

Mrs. Gotz blanched and took a step back, her hand rising again to her throat, her fingers fluttering like butterfly wings. "To where?"

"The Barstow farm, ma'am," Sergeant Macon said. "Leroy Barstow has deserted and I've been sent to fetch him back."

Ira Spivey and Mrs. Gotz swapped looks, and Spivey said guardedly, "You don't say. What makes you think he would come back here?"

"Jaflyn is his home," Sergeant Macon said. "Nine times out of ten, that's where deserters head. I need to question his parents."

"His father is long dead," Ira Spivey revealed. "Shot when Leroy was ten years old." He seemed to catch himself and hastily amended, "It was a hunting accident. The mother has run the farm by herself ever since."

"What is the mother's name?" Sergeant Macon inquired in his newfound polite manner.

"You don't know?" Mrs. Gotz responded. "Martha. Martha Barstow. As kind a woman as ever lived. The things she has had to put up with—" Mrs. Gotz raised her hand to her mouth and gave a short laugh that came out more like a bark. "Listen to me, running off so. I had better be careful."

"Is her farm near yours?"

"Oh, goodness, no. Go north a ways until you come to a road that leads west. The Barstow place is ten miles out. You'll come to a fork. Go south until you come to some hills. Their cabin is back there in those hills."

"Thank you, ma'am," Macon said, and surprised Fargo by gently taking the woman's good hand and giving it a squeeze. "We are grateful for your help." He placed his hat back on, touched the brim to Spivey, and made for the street.

Fargo waited until they were outside to ask, "What was that all about? You did more talking in there than you did the whole time we were on the trail."

"My grandmother used to say you can catch more flies with molasses than you can with arsenic," Sergeant Macon remarked. Hooking his boot in his mount's stirrup, he swung up. "I've found that when I'm tracking a deserter down, I get better results being nice than bashing heads."

"Barstow isn't the first one you've gone after?"

"Where did you get that idea?" Sergeant Macon rejoined. "By my reckoning he'll be the sixty-fifth. You might say hunting deserters is my specialty. I've been doing it for pretty near twenty years now. When Colonel Crane sent for me, I came straightaway." He paused. "I usually work alone. But in your case I've made an exception."

Fargo was learning more by the second. "Why?"

"If I had been in your boots, I would want Barstow held to account as much as you do."

"I've never wanted anything more," Fargo said.

"Maybe it will make you feel a little less guilty about the girl if you help bring her murderer to justice."

The comment gave Fargo a whole new insight into his companion. There was a lot more to Macon than met the eye. "You talk like someone who has been through the same thing."

"Close to it," Sergeant Macon said. "Back when I was a raw recruit, a drunk private shot the lieutenant I was serving under. As decent an officer as you would ever meet, killed because he caught the trooper passed out from too much whiskey while on guard duty, and was going to clap him in irons. I volunteered to go after him and the major let me because he couldn't spare anyone else. That's how I got my start."

Fargo forked leather and they rode toward the

north end of Jaflyn. Once again faces peered at them through dusty window panes. They were abreast of a frame house in need of paint and repairs to its sagging roof when an urchin of ten or twelve appeared at the corner of an overgrown hedge. The boy wore torn, faded pants, and nothing more. Grime streaked his face and bare feet.

Macon oozed more molasses. "Is the fishing good hereabouts, son?"

Instead of answering, the boy glanced up and down the street as if fearful of being overheard. "Are you after him?"

"Him who?" Sergeant Macon asked.

"The bad man. The one everyone is so scared of." The boy looked over his shoulder at the house. "Even my ma and pa."

Fargo reined up. "Does this bad man have a name?"

"Leroy," the boy said, barely loud enough for them to hear. "But don't tell anyone I told you. I'll get a licking."

"Leroy Barstow?" Sergeant Macon said.

"That's him, sure enough," the boy confirmed. "The Devil, folks call him. I shouldn't be telling you this, but they say he's fixing to shoot every last one of us like he did all those others."

Fargo assumed the boy was referring to the survey detail. "How did you hear about that?"

Sergeant Macon had a question of his own. "Have you seen the Devil recently, son? Say, in the past few weeks?"

The boy chose to answer Macon. "I've seen him several times since he came back. He wore a uniform a lot like yours when he first showed up but now he wears the same clothes as everyone else."

Fargo pulsed with eagerness. So Barstow *was* there,

and it was only a matter of finding exactly where. "Have you talked to him?"

"To the Devil?" the boy said, and laughed. "Mister, I'd have to be crazy to do that. He shoots people for no reason."

"What's your name, son?" Sergeant Macon asked.

The boy hesitated.

"I promise not to tell a soul," Macon assured him.

"Tommy. Tommy Hinmet. My pa runs the stable but there's never much business."

"Well, Tommy. You have my personal guarantee that Leroy Barstow won't shoot anyone ever again once I take him into custody. Help us, and there's a reward in it for you."

"A reward?" the boy said uncertainly.

"Money," Sergeant Macon explained. "Fifty dollars to do with as you please. All you need do is supply information that will lead to Barstow's apprehension and incarceration."

The boy's eyes had about bugged out of his head at the mention of the sum. "What do I have to do to earn it? What did all those fancy words mean?"

His saddle creaking, Sergeant Macon bent toward the hedge. "All you have to do is tell us where we can find him."

"That's all?"

Macon nodded, then shifted and patted his saddle-bags. "I have the fifty dollars right here. Will you help us?"

Before the boy could answer, a scarecrow of a woman in a threadbare dress stepped from the house. "What are you two doing there?" she demanded suspiciously. "Who are you talking to?"

Tommy had ducked down the instant the door opened. Putting a finger to his lips, he vigorously shook his head.

"Just to each other, ma'am," Sergeant Macon lied. "We'll move on if we're bothering you." He smiled and clucked to his horse.

Fargo did likewise. He noticed that the woman's left hand was crippled, her fingers twisted and splayed.

"Don't you worry," Tommy Hinmet whispered as they went by. "I'll find out where the Devil is hiding and let you know, if it's the last thing I ever do."

13

The road was a dirt track furrowed by the ruts of wagon wheels and pockmarked with hoofprints. It wound across the rolling farmland like a sinuous snake. Here and there stood scattered farmhouses and barns. Islands of vegetation broke the sameness of the sea of swaying grass. The wind was strong, and far to the northwest a dark smear represented the leading edge of a cloud bank.

The rabbit population was booming. Fargo counted six in the first couple of miles. He also spotted grazing deer, a pair of red hawks with their wings outstretched, and various songbirds on the wing.

Five miles out of Jaflyn they encountered a rider coming the other way. A stocky farmer, distinguished by his overalls and general appearance, drew rein and greeted them with a thickly accented, "Greetings to you, friends."

Fargo was going to ride on by but Sergeant Macon came to a stop and leaned on his saddle horn.

"Pleased to make your acquaintance, mister." Macon revealed who he was. "I take it you have a farm nearby?"

"Yes, sir," the man answered. He seemed to be greatly impressed by the sergeant's uniform. "Just over there." He pointed in the direction of the clouds. "I am Mikolaj Klimas."

"Polish, unless I'm mistaken," Sergeant Macon said.

"Yes. I came from Poland with my family two years ago to make new home in America." Mikolaj said it with a certain degree of sadness.

"You are not happy here?"

"We were very happy. Once." Mikolaj shook himself and lifted his reins. "I am sorry. I have business in town."

"One thing," Sergeant Macon said, holding out his arm. "You must know Martha Barstow."

Mikolaj would make a terrible poker player. His face mirrored his every emotion. At the moment it reflected great wariness. "Yes. I know her. A fine woman. She has been to our house several times to visit my wife. My wife can not get out much. She has a bad leg."

"You must know her son, too. Leroy."

For a few seconds budding rage contorted Mikolaj's countenance. Struggling to stay calm, he answered sullenly, "Yes."

"Have you talked to him recently?"

"Pardon?" Mikolaj said.

"In the past couple of weeks or so?" Sergeant Macon said. "He has deserted from the army and I have been sent to take him back."

The sun and Mikolaj's face were one and the same. "You have?" He could scarcely contain his joy. "That is good. That is very good."

"So have you seen him or not?"

Just like that, the gloom returned. "No, sir. I have not seen him since he went away about a year ago."

Fargo suspected the farmer was lying. Macon had to suspect it, too, but he did not let on.

"I won't detain you, then. Have a nice day, Mr. Klimas. And if you should run across Leroy Barstow, leave word for me at the general store."

"I will do that," the farmer said, but it was as plain

as the fact that he could not look them in the eyes that he would do no such thing.

Fargo watched the man ride off. Something was pricking at the back of his mind, but he could not say what, or why. It puzzled him.

"Interesting how everyone thinks so highly of the mother," Sergeant Macon commented. "I look forward to meeting her."

The fork was right where Mrs. Gotz had said it would be. They rode south, and in due course the hills she had mentioned reared ahead. Dark hills, thick with timber, mostly pine, and sprinkled liberally with boulders.

Macon scratched his chin. "I wonder why the Barstows don't have their farm out on the grassland like the rest?"

"Maybe they liked to be by themselves."

The road became little more than a path. Shadowy timber bordered both sides. Strangely silent timber, with few signs of wildlife.

Fargo rode with his hand on his Colt. He was in the lead, rounding a bend, when the Ovaro snorted and shied. He had the Colt half out of its holster before he realized the pinto had been spooked by a dead buck. It lay a few feet off the path, its tongue jutting from its mouth. Flies buzzed about the head and crawled in and out of the mouth, nose, and ears. A bullet hole testified to the cause of death.

"That buck hasn't been dead long," Sergeant Macon said. "The scavengers haven't been at it yet."

Fargo dismounted. He gripped a foreleg and shook it. The buck was as stiff as a board and gave off a distinct order. The body was beginning to bloat. "Several days, at least."

"Why would a hunter shoot it and not take the meat?"

Fargo had no idea. He climbed back on the Ovaro. Not ten yards farther they came on a remarkable sight.

Two dead coyotes on the same side of the path as the buck. And like the buck, each had been shot in the head. They had not been otherwise touched.

"Damned peculiar," Sergeant Macon remarked.

Fargo turned in the saddle, thinking out loud. "They caught the buck's scent and came to help themselves. But whoever shot the buck was waiting, and shot them, too."

"And left all three lying there? Who would do—?" Sergeant Macon stopped. "Dear God. You told me he likes to kill, but I had no idea."

Fargo was scanning the trees. He had that feeling again, the feeling of being watched. Gigging the Ovaro, he threaded deeper into the hills. Half a mile more, and they came to a flat area roughly five acres in extent. In the center sat a cabin and a barn. Both were dilapidated. Signs of neglect were everywhere: in the chinks in the logs, in the cracked windows, in the stable door that hung by one hinge. Smoke curled sluggishly from the chimney.

"Someone is home." Sergeant Macon shucked his carbine from his saddle scabbard and inserted a cartridge into the chamber.

Spreading out, they cautiously approached. Suddenly Fargo tensed. From inside came the unmistakable sound of a woman weeping. They reined up, and Macon slid down and cautiously stepped to the cabin door. He knocked lightly.

The weeping abruptly stopped. Over a minute went by, and Macon was about to knock again when the door opened a few inches. Enough for whoever had opened it to see out but not enough for them to see in.

"Yes?" the woman asked, almost fearfully.

"Mrs. Barstow?" Sergeant Bacon took off his hat and lowered his carbine. "Sorry to disturb you, ma'am, but I imagine you can guess why I'm here."

The door opened all the way.

For as long as he lived, Fargo would never forget his first sight of Martha Barstow. She was sorrow personified. Even though she looked to be in her mid to late forties, her hair was as white as driven snow. Even her eyebrows were white. She was thin to the point of emaciation, and stood stooped over, as if the weight of the world were on her slim shoulders. A faded blue shawl was draped over them and the upper third of a well-worn gray dress that clung to her in folds, hinting she had lost a lot of weight. But it was her face that indelibly impressed him: an unhealthy pallor, dark shadows under both eyes, and sunken cheeks that lent her an air of the deepest sorrow. She had dried her face, or tried to. Partial streaks of tears glistened. "Yes, I can guess. You are here after my son." Her voice was as soft as cotton and as sorrowful as a shattered heart.

"Is he here?" Sergeant Macon asked.

"No. He had business to attend to and won't be back for days." Martha stepped aside. "Would you care to come in? I have coffee on the stove if you're of a mind to have some."

Macon smiled and motioned. "After you, Mrs. Barstow."

Fargo surveyed the surrounding hills. He wondered if the woman was lying. Everyone claimed she was as decent as the year was long, but she was also Leroy's mother, and motherly love might compel her to do things she otherwise would not. With a start, he realized she had not gone in, and was staring at him.

"My invite applies to you too, mister."

"I'm obliged." Alighting, Fargo followed them. Since the windows were closed and the burlap curtains pulled, it was like stepping into a cave. He paused to let his eyes adjust. There were a table and chairs that had seen better days, a settee with more scrapes and scuff marks than a five-year-old, and a butter churn.

That was it. Judging by appearances, the Barstows were as poor as dirt.

"I've been expecting someone to show up," Martha commented as she went to a shelf near a stone fireplace and took down a lamp. She placed it in the center of the table, then patted two chairs. "Don't stand on ceremony. Have a seat. I'll bring your coffee directly."

"Take your time," Sergeant Macon said, and sank into a chair with his broad back to the front door.

Not Fargo. He liked to have his back to a wall, especially when there was a chance someone might use it for target practice or stick a knife between his shoulder blades. "Does your son have a new rifle?"

"Yes, as matter of fact. A pretty thing. All shiny and brass."

Fargo's Henry. He had more questions but Sergeant Macon beat him to it.

"Mrs. Barstow, we need to know all you can tell us about his whereabouts. He has murdered twenty-two people and must be held to account."

"Twenty-two?" Martha repeated. "If only it were that few. No, I would say the tally is closer to sixty."

Fargo was not sure he had heard her correctly. "How can it be that many? You must be mistaken."

Martha looked at him, her eyes moistening. "I wish to God I was. But it's not such a great lot when you consider Leroy has been killing folks since he was seven."

To judge by Macon's expression, he was as astounded as Fargo. "Ma'am, if you don't mind, I would appreciate the details."

The wick in the lamp was aglow. Martha stepped back from the table and smoothed her dress. "Very well. I suppose it's time someone knew the whole story. But first, can I interest either of you gentlemen in soup and crackers? I'm afraid it's all I have to offer."

Fargo spoke for both of them, answering, "We're not hungry."

Sergeant Macon was studying the mother. "How is it you have so little when so much game is to be had? Why, just down the trail a short way is a prime buck going to waste."

"That was my son's doing," Martha said. "He didn't kill it for the meat. He killed it for the sake of killing it. That's how he's always been." She opened a cupboard and brought over two chipped china cups. Taking a ripped towel from the counter, she folded it so she could use it to grip the handle of the coffeepot without being burned. She filled both cups and set the pot back on the stove. "I'm sorry, but I don't have any milk, and I've been out of sugar for months."

"I like my coffee black," Sergeant Macon said.

Martha smiled thinly and finally sat. She placed her scrawny elbows on the edge of the table and leaned on them as if weary to her core. "It's nice to have visitors. I haven't had company since forever."

"Folks don't like to come this far out?" Macon prompted.

Her laugh was warm but brittle. "Not if they want to go on living. My son might take it into his head to shoot them, and then where would they be?"

Fargo tried his coffee. It was weak but it would do. "What was that about Leroy has been killing since he was seven?"

"As God is my witness," Martha said. "The first ones were his grandmother and grandfather. He was spending the night with them, and he got mad when they wouldn't let him stay up past his bedtime. So that night when they were asleep, he snuck into the kitchen, helped himself to a carving knife, and stabbed them in the throats while they slept."

Sergeant Macon posed the very thing uppermost on Fargo's own mind. "Begging your pardon, ma'am, but

115

why is it there is no record of those murders? Or all the others you claim your son committed?"

"I will get to the others shortly. As for my husband's parents, he didn't want the boy taken from us. So he made me promise to never tell a soul. Their deaths were blamed on robbers."

"Did this happen in Minnesota?"

"No, sir. Back in Ohio, where we are from originally. We had to leave because once Leroy took to killing, he couldn't stop. He pushed a neighbor girl down a well, threw a small boy off a hayloft and broke the boy's neck, that sort of thing."

"Hold on a second, ma'am," Sergeant Macon said. "How is it he wasn't ever caught?"

"My Leroy has always been clever like a fox." Martha was stating a fact, not bragging. "All the deaths were considered accidents."

"How many did he murder before you left Ohio?" Fargo asked.

Martha pondered a few seconds. "Eleven, I reckon, although there might have been a few more my husband and me didn't know about."

Sergeant Macon was incredulous. "You let him go on killing? How is it that you didn't turn him over to the authorities?"

"He was our son," Martha said simply. "We loved him, and we kept hoping for the better. Besides, Leroy would have killed me like he did my husband if I said a word to anyone."

"I'm having a hard time taking all of this in," Sergeant Macon said.

Martha smiled. "Don't fret yourself over the past. It's the here and now you need to be concerned with."

"In what way?" Fargo inquired when she did not go on.

"My son plans to kill the two of you, too."

14

In the silence that descended, Fargo could have heard a feather flutter to the floor. He broke the silence by saying, "Your son told you that for a fact? And called us by name?"

"Oh, no," Martha said. "He just told me that he was sure the army would send someone to fetch him back, and when they got here, he aimed to kill them. Then he plans to chop off a few fingers and send the fingers to the army as a warning to leave him be."

"Does he honestly think the army will give up just like that?" Sergeant Macon asked, snapping his fingers. "It's preposterous."

"Leroy has always used killing to get his way. I reckon he figures it will work with the army, too."

Fargo sipped coffee, debating what to ask next. "Tell us more about the people you say he's murdered. Your husband was one of them?"

Martha nodded. "About a year after we moved here. Clovis, that was my husband's name, got fed up with Leroy's bloodletting. Leroy was doing the same thing here that he had done in Ohio. He stabbed a boy out behind the general store and claimed the boy was playing with the knife and fell on it. He pushed old Mrs. Festle into the path of a wagon when no one was looking. Those sorts of things."

"All in Jaflyn?" Macon said.

"Oh, no. Leroy likes to wander, and he kills everywhere he goes." Martha paused. "One evening Clovis sat the boy down at this very table and lit into him, saying as how we moved here to start a new life, and the killing had to end. The next morning, bright and early, Clovis went out to milk the cows, as he usually did. When he didn't come back in an hour or so, I went out to see why." Martha's torment at the memory was transparent. "I found my husband on his belly with the pitchfork buried in his back."

"Dear God."

"Leroy came up to me while I was standing there and yanked the pitchfork out," Martha continued her account. "He held it up to my face, the tines dripping blood, and told me that if I didn't behave, he would do the same to me as he had done to Clovis."

"His own mother," Macon said softly.

"Kin don't make any never mind to him," Martha said. "He'll kill anyone at the drop of a hat, and drop the hat himself."

"So you never went to the law," Fargo said, unable to keep the reproach out of his tone.

"No, mister, I didn't. I wanted to. I went out to the stable a few times, thinking I would saddle up and go report him. But I couldn't bring myself to do it. Not out of love, because by then I didn't much care whether Leroy lived or died. No, I couldn't do it because I was afraid. I knew what he was capable of. I guess when all is said and done, I'm a coward at heart."

"No one can blame you for being scared," Sergeant Macon said.

"They don't need to. I blame myself every second of every minute of every day of every week of the whole year," Martha said. "I can't tell you how happy I was when that judge in Mankato had him shipped off to the army. I thought at long last it was over."

Martha bowed her head. "I should have known better."

"The business in Mankato had something to do with a girl, I've been told," Sergeant Macon mentioned.

"Leroy's sugarplum. Or that is what he calls her. He says he loves her, and wants to marry her but her parents don't want her to have anything to do with him."

"How does the girl feel about it?" Fargo asked.

"She wants to be shed of Leroy. But that's not likely to happen. Once my boy sets his mind to something, he's hard to shake."

"I'll want to look her up," Sergeant Macon said. "Where in Mankato does she live?"

"She doesn't," Martha said. "She lives on her parents' farm outside of Jaflyn. The Gotz farm. Patricia is her name."

"We met her mother!" Macon exclaimed. "She never mentioned her daughter was involved with your son."

"Who can blame her?" Martha said. "Would you want your daughter to take up with a killer?"

"Where does Mankato fit in?" Fargo had it all worked out except for that. Or thought he did.

"It's where court is held," Martha enlightened him. "Judge Renwick presides. He's the one who gave Leroy the choice of jail or the army." She absently swiped at a limp bang. "Leroy hates Renwick. He's on his way to Mankato right this moment to kill him."

Fargo and Sergeant Macon both said, "What?" at the same instant. Macon added, "Why didn't you tell us this sooner? Your son has to be stopped." The sergeant rose. "How much of a head start does he have?"

"Leroy left yesterday about ten in the morning," Martha revealed. "It will be a waste of your time to go after him. He's there by now, and by morning Judge

119

Renwick will be dead. You have no hope of reaching Mankato in time."

"Let us be the judge of that." Sergeant Macon wheeled. "Coming?" he said to Fargo.

Fargo stayed in his chair. As reluctant as he was to admit it, Martha Barstow was right. Her son had too much of a lead. They could not reach Mankato before the judge was added to Leroy's long list of victim. He said as much.

"We still have to try," Macon insisted. "A man's life is at stake."

"What good would it do to ride our horses into the ground for someone who is already worm food?" Fargo argued. "We should stay here and wait for Leroy to return." He glanced at Martha. "He is coming back, isn't he?"

"Oh, yes. He goes away for a few days now and again but he always comes home. He has no place else. I'm all he has left in the world."

Fargo felt no sympathy whatsoever. Her son was a rabid wolf, a kill-crazy madman who would not stop slaughtering innocents this side of the grave.

Sergeant Macon had reached the front door and was fingering the latch. "Now that I think about it, maybe it's wiser if we split up. I'll ride to Mankato to warn the judge, just in case Leroy is delayed in doing the deed. You stay here and keep your eyes peeled, and if he shows up, nab him. Agreed?"

It was fine by Fargo. "Just one thing," he said. "I'll try to take him alive. But if it comes down to him or me, it won't be me."

"Fair enough. Good luck." Macon flew out to his horse. He left the door open, and through it Fargo saw him apply his spurs.

"I reckon it's just you and me now," Martha said. "Are you sure I can't interest you in that soup?"

"I'm more interested in why something hasn't been

done about your son long before now," Fargo said. "From what I can gather, everyone in Jaflyn knows about him. Why haven't they banded together and put an end to it?"

"They're afraid."

"There has to be more to it than that," Fargo disagreed. Five or six men with rifles were all it would take. They could lie in ambush near the Barstow house and wait for Leroy to ride into their gun sights.

"Have you been to Jaflyn?" Martha asked.

"Before we came here. Why?"

"Did you notice anything unusual about the people?"

Puzzled, Fargo responded, "Not that I recollect. We didn't meet everyone, just Spivey at the general store and Mrs. Gotz and a woman down the street." He stopped, jarred by the recollection of something all three had in common: Spivey with his useless leg, Mrs. Gotz with her useless arm, the other woman with her crippled hand. He mentioned them to Martha.

"How do you think they got that way?"

"Accidents. Spivey took a bad fall. Mrs. Gotz was kicked by a horse."

"They lied. The only accident that befell all three of them was my son. He shot them."

"All three?"

"And more besides. Not to kill, mind you. But as a warning and a lesson. Whenever he hears that someone is speaking out against him, he pays them a visit. It's why the people in Jaflyn have never formed a vigilance committee and treated my son to a strangulation jig. They call him the Devil, and they are as afraid of him as they would be of the real Satan."

Fargo digested the revelation with a sense of horror. One person, a mere youth, held an entire settlement in a grip of terror. "How many has he crippled?"

"I can't rightly say. He doesn't always tell me.

121

Sometimes he'll ride off and be gone a few days, and later I'll hear about someone who has had an accident. I always know better, and so does everyone else."

"You never had a chance to end it? Not in all these years?"

"I told you. I'm just like everyone else. I'm deathly afraid of him. And like I've said, he's clever. He bolts his bedroom door at night. Or goes to sleep out under the stars where no one can find him. He gives me money and has me buy anything he needs from Jaflyn. Never any for me, mind you."

Her extreme poverty sparked another question. "Where does he get all this money from?"

"He doesn't ever say and I don't ever ask. The last time I got curious, he shot the dog I had."

Fargo sat back. In all his experience he had never encountered anything like this. It changed things. He had to rethink his promises to Colonel Crane and Sergeant Macon.

"Like I keep saying, Leroy is real clever. When he gets an urge to kill, he'll go find a stranger. He roams all over on his hunts, as he calls them. As far north as Minneapolis, as far east as Wisconsin."

"And the law hasn't take notice of all the dead people?" To Fargo it was too incredible to be believed.

"Most of Leroy's victims just up and disappear. Usually the Sioux are blamed, leaving Leroy free to go on with his killing."

"Yet he was hauled before a judge for trifling with Patricia Gotz," Fargo said in disgust.

"It was not exactly a trifle. She was in the family way. Since she was thirteen, Mr. Gotz filed a complaint. He had always objected to Leroy courting his daughter. Then one night, as Mrs. Gotz was coming out of their barn, someone shot her in the arm. No one saw Leroy do it but it was him, sure enough." Martha sighed. "Anyway, the county sheriff showed up here one morning when Leroy was still abed. The sheriff waited right at this table, and when Leroy came out, arrested him without any fuss."

Fargo was more interested in something else. "Patricia Gotz is going to have Leroy's baby?"

"Not anymore. Mr. Gotz took her east. They were gone about a month. When they came back Patricia was no longer in the family way."

"Gotz sounds like the only man in the community with backbone," Fargo observed.

"He was, yes."

"Was?"

"Leroy was released on bail. He was mad, as you can imagine. So mad, he stormed around here cursing Mr. Gotz to high heaven. He left for a few days. Shortly after he got back, I was in town and heard that Mr. Gotz was clearing some ground and a tree fell on him. He was crushed to death."

"No one suspected your son?"

"Sure they did. But they couldn't prove anything. Leroy was too slick, as always. He told me how he did it. He snuck up behind Gotz while Gotz was chopping the tree and hit him over the head with a rock. Then he placed Gotz right where the tree was bound to fall, and finished chopping it down himself. Leroy said I should have heard the bones crack and crunch."

Fargo wondered about something. "Why are you telling me all this, Mrs. Barstow? Aren't you afraid I'll go to the sheriff?"

"You won't. It would be your word against my son's, and without proof, there's nothing the sheriff can do."

"You could testify against him," Fargo proposed.

"I'm sorry. No. I want to go on living. Mother or no, Leroy would not hesitate to kill me if I turned against him. Out in the open, that is."

"I'm not sure I follow you."

Martha bent toward him. Her features burned with intensity. "I can't live like this any longer. Always being afraid. Never knowing when he'll do to me like he did to his pa and his grandparents. And sick in my heart over all the other people he has murdered. Men, women, children. He smothered a baby once. Snuck into a house while the mother was out hanging up laundry, and covered the baby's mouth and nose with a pillow."

Fargo had tangled with killers of every description. Apaches who tortured prisoners to test their mettle. Outlaws who would shoot anyone who glanced at them crosswise. Cutthroats who would stick a blade into someone for a few measly dollars. None could hold a candle to farm boy Leroy Barstow when it came to pure mean viciousness. Leroy had no conscience, no sense of right and wrong. In Leroy's eyes, taking a human life was no different than squashing a bug.

Sure, Apaches indulged in torture, but they were good providers for their wives and devoted fathers to their children. Sure, outlaws were quick on the trigger, but most had loved ones they cared for. Sure, river rats would stick a blade into a man for a paltry poke, but they, too, usually had families and friends. Leroy was different. Leroy cared about no one but Leroy. He had no good traits whatsoever.

Fargo became aware that Martha had gone on.

"I'm telling you all this because I want it to end. The sergeant wants to take my son back alive. But you don't. I can see it in your eyes." Martha reached across the table and clasped Fargo's hand. "I'm begging you. Kill him. Kill my son for me and put an end to it all."

Fargo was about to reply when cackling laughter brought him to his feet and caused Martha to cry out in fear.

15

Fargo's first impulse was to dash to the door and fling it open. On the verge of doing so, he froze. Rushing out might be just what the young killer wanted him to do. Palming his Colt, he sidled to a window and carefully parted the burlap curtain. The window was so dirty it was like peering into a dust storm.

"As I live and breathe!" Leroy Barstow hollered from somewhere on the north side of the cabin. "Is that you in there with my ma, scout? I remember this pinto of yours."

Since it was pointless to deny it, Fargo shouted, "It's me, boy."

"My, oh my. Now what would bring a great scout like you all the way to Minnesota to visit little ol' me?"

"You have a lot to answer for."

"It's lucky for me, then, that you left your horse out where anyone could see it," Leroy taunted. "Otherwise, I might have walked right on in and found myself looking down the barrel of your gun. And I wouldn't want that."

Martha was clutching her throat with one hand and the edge of the table with the other. "This can't be," she mewed. She quaked like an aspen leaf in a stiff wind, then yelled, "Leroy, this is your ma! I thought you were in Mankato!"

When Leroy answered, he appeared to be closer to

the cabin. "I met a man on the road who told me the judge has gone back east to visit kin and won't be back for a week or more, so I came home."

"Did you just get here?"

Leroy uttered a loud snort. "What a strange thing for a mother to ask. Can it be you're not happy to have the flesh of your flesh back home?"

"Of course I am, son," Martha said much too quickly. "It's just that I was taken by surprise, is all."

"I'll bet." Again Leroy's voice came from a different spot. "It can't be that you're worried about what I might have done to that sergeant who rode off a while ago, can it?"

Fargo gave a start. He had assumed Sergeant Macon was well on his way, and well out of danger.

Martha moved to the door and pressed her cheek to it. "Not again, Leroy. Please tell me you haven't shot him."

"Why, Ma? Would I do a thing like that?" Leroy cackled. He was close to the front. "But you can set your mind at ease. I didn't put a window in his skull." Leroy snickered. "I did something better."

"Oh, son," Martha said.

Fargo was straining to catch sight of her offspring but the wily killer kept out of sight of the window.

"Why are you so upset? You don't even know what I did," Leroy complained. "But it's one of my best yet, Ma. I only wish I could be there to see the look on his face when it happens."

Gliding to the door, Fargo whispered, "Keep him talking. Draw him in close. I have a plan." Such as it was.

Martha nodded and loudly asked, "When what happens, son? Did you pull another of your tricks?"

When Leroy answered he was closer than ever, no more than six or seven feet from the door.

"I came in by the back trail, Ma. I was almost here

126

when I saw Fargo and the sergeant ride up. I moved around to where I could see their horses better, thinking I would make buzzard bait of them as they came out. But then I had a brainstorm."

"I'm listening," Martha said.

"You'll love this one, Ma. You truly will." Leroy had to be right outside. "Do you remember that gully yonder? The one where we always find the snakes?"

Martha stared aghast at Fargo. "Lord, no."

"I ran there and started turning rocks over, and sure enough, in no time I found me a small one." Leroy was quite pleased with himself and it showed in his voice. "I stuck it in the sergeant's saddlebags. When he opens them, he's in for a surprise."

Fargo suspected what the answer would be but he asked anyway, "What kind of snake is he talking about?"

"A rattler," Martha whispered. "On hot days that gully is always crawling with them."

"Are you proud of me, Ma?" Leroy was enjoying himself. "Don't you agree it's one of my best ever?"

The scheme was pure wickedness. Rattlesnakes did not always shake their rattles before they struck. Young rattlesnakes were even less prone to do so since their rattles were not fully formed. Sergeant Macon would reach into his saddlebags for his coffee or something else, and be bitten. Some people thought that the venom of young rattlers was less potent than the venom of older snakes but that was not true. The venom of the young snakes was every bit as deadly.

Fargo had to warn Macon. He motioned for Martha to back away from the door, and lightly gripped the latch.

"Ma? Why don't you answer me?"

Martha cleared her throat and called out, "Sorry, son. Yes, it is one of your best yet. But I can't help feeling sorry for that poor soldier."

"You always have been too kindhearted for your own damn good," Leroy criticized. "You need to be more like me."

Fargo was ready. He yanked on the door and threw himself out, crouching and extending the Colt, ready to shoot the instant he set eyes on Barstow. He figured Leroy was to his right, and he was right. But he did not shoot. His trigger finger started to curl but he did not apply enough pressure to squeeze the trigger. He couldn't. The young killer has outfoxed him.

Leroy was behind the Ovaro. Only part of him was visible: the part that was holding the muzzle of Fargo's Henry to the Ovaro's head. "Go ahead, scout," Leroy goaded. "Maybe you'll drop me before I drop your horse and maybe you won't."

Part of Fargo roared at him to shoot, that the pinto was only an animal. But another part of him could not do it. He had ridden the Ovaro for years. Together they had endured heat and cold and thirst and hunger. They had been caught in blizzards, swept by sandstorms, faced death a hundred and one times, and survived. He let the Colt drop.

Leroy chuckled and stepped into the open, leveling the Henry at Fargo as he did. "Well, now. That was easier than I thought it would be. You're willing to die for a stupid horse?"

"You would never understand," Fargo said.

"I suppose not. But it is a right fine animal. I might keep it for myself once I'm done with you." Leroy wagged the Henry. "Step over here with your arms above your head."

Fargo did as he was told. He still had the Arkansas toothpick in its ankle sheath. Maybe, just maybe, Leroy would be careless and give him a chance to bury it in the bloodthirsty bastard's heart.

"That's far enough," Leroy said, then craned his neck to one side. "Ma? You come on out here, too."

Martha complied, her features a mask of despair. She moved slowly, shuffling her legs, nearly all the vitality drained out of her. She was on the brink of emotional and physical collapse. "What now, son? Will you kill us like you have all those others?"

Leroy recoiled as if she had kicked him. "Make worm food of my own mother? What kind of person do you take me for?"

A derisive snort spilled from Fargo before he could stop it. Leroy flushed and sighted down the Henry's barrel.

"I know exactly what kind of person you are, son," Martha said tiredly. "You are an ogre. A monster. The Devil, folks call you, and that's as good a description as any. You have no conscience, son. I suspect you might not even have a soul."

"That's plain silly," Leroy said, but there was something in his tone, a hint of hurt at his mother's condemnation.

"I have always been honest with you, son," Martha said. "I am being truthful now when I say that if you murder this man, I will never speak to you again."

Leroy started to laugh but stopped. "You're serious?"

"Never more so. I just can't take it anymore. The cost is more than one human being can bear."

"What cost?" Leroy asked. "I've never laid a finger on you. Not once my whole life long."

"You don't need to. It's all the people you've killed. Including your own pa, son. Your own pa! I always knew you would do the same to me one day. Time and again I have prayed for the strength to do what must be done, and time and again I have found myself lacking. That's the only reason I am still alive."

Fargo marveled at her boldness. She had her head in a bear trap. The wrong word, and the trap would snap shut.

"That's not true, Ma," Leroy said. "You have always been special to me."

"Not special enough for you to do as I have asked and stop the killing or turn yourself in." Martha ran a hand across her eyes. "I have reached the point where I honestly don't care if I live or die."

Leroy lowered the Henry, but only a few inches. "If you don't want me to shoot him in front of you, I won't."

The reprieve, however temporary, gave Fargo cause for hope. The longer he was kept alive, the higher the odds of him somehow turning the tables.

"For you, Ma, I'll give him a fighting chance," Leroy said. "If he escapes, he lives. If he doesn't, well"—Leroy shrugged—"you can't say I wasn't fair."

Martha appeared stunned. "You would do that for me?"

"For the woman who brought me into this world? Sure." Leroy bestowed an oily smile on Fargo. "How to go about this? I know! Ma, fetch that rope off his saddle. But first get a knife out of the cabin."

Martha hesitated. "You won't kill him the moment my back is turned? You give me your solemn word?"

"May God strike me dead if I do." Leroy waited until the door had closed behind her, then winked at Fargo and whispered, "Just between you and me, that woman is as dumb as a stump."

"I didn't think you meant it," Fargo said.

"Oh, but I do! I haven't shot you yet, have I? It just won't be quite as fair as she's expecting. After all, I can't have you getting away, now can I?"

"You can't keep this up forever," Fargo mentioned. "Killing Sergeant Macon and me won't help you any. The army will send others to take our places. Sooner or later they will catch you."

"This might surprise you, scout, but I agree. And I've been giving some thought to what to do. Do you remember Private Weaver? Well, he told me that a cousin of his got in trouble with the law and had to skip the U.S. one step ahead of a noose. The cousin went to South America. Ever hear of it?"

Fargo allowed that he had.

"Weaver said his cousin was safe down there because the country the cousin went to doesn't have a"—Leroy stopped, his brow knitting—"what did he call it? An extra-something-or-other. Anyway, once I get there, the army can raise all the fuss it wants but there is nothing they can do."

The awful thing was, Fargo realized, Leroy was right. The long arm of U.S. law could not touch him in a country that did not have an extradition treaty with the United States.

"Pretty smart of me, huh?" Leroy crowed. "But it gets even better. Weaver told me that some places down there are so wild and remote, a gent could lose himself in them forever. And there's hardly any law to speak of. I can go on doing what I like to do best for the rest of my natural days."

Fargo had heard the same thing about South America. Much of it was jungle sprinkled with small villages. For the most part, the natives were friendly and easygoing, which made them ripe for the slaughter. "I've never met anyone like you."

Leroy took that as a compliment. "Ma keeps saying I'm one of a kind. But hell. Indians kill people all the time. I'm not much different than they are."

"Indians kill to count coup on their enemies," Fargo clarified. "You kill because you love killing."

"That's not entirely true. I always have a good reason. Take that old he-goat, Mountain Joe. I snuck over to the lean-to looking for his daughter and saw him sleeping, with no one else around. It had been so long since I killed, I couldn't stop myself."

"You call that a reason?"

"You've killed, haven't you?" Leroy asked.

"Only when I had to," Fargo answered, wondering what that had to do with anything.

"Then you must know what it is like. The thrill. The excitement. Ever seen how pretty blood is when it gushes? Or felt your fingers dig deep into soft flesh as you throttled the life from someone?" Leroy licked his thin lips. "There's nothing like it."

If Fargo had any lingering doubts that Leroy Barstow was insane, they were now shattered.

The front door opened. Martha reappeared holding a butcher knife. Leroy directed her to remove the rope from Fargo's saddle, then cut two pieces about a foot and a half long. Martha balked at his next instruction; she was to bind Fargo's arms and legs.

"If you don't," Leroy said, "I'll shoot him and be done with all this bother."

Martha bent over Fargo's forearms. "I'm truly sorry." She looped one of the ropes around his wrists.

"Make them good and tight, Ma," Leroy cautioned. "And don't think I won't check that you do."

It took Martha a while. She fumbled with the ropes, had to retie several knots. Fargo suspected she was stalling for his benefit, but eventually she stepped back.

"Don't move, scout." Leroy stepped up close and gouged the Henry's muzzle into Fargo's gut. Then, one-handed, he tugged at Fargo's bonds. "Not bad," he praised his mother. Moving away, he smiled and gestured at the thickly wooded hills that encircled the clearing. "Ready to play bunny?"

"Bunny?" Fargo repeated quizzically.

"As in bunny rabbit. It's a game I've just invented. The rules are simple. You start hopping as fast as you can. I will count to one hundred, then come after you and blow your brains out." Leroy smirked. "Any questions before we begin? No? Then off you go, little rabbit."

16

Fargo did not waste time bandying words. Taking giant hops, he bounded toward the woods. He had to be careful not to lean too far to either side or he would fall. It helped that his hands were tied in front of him and not behind. Leroy had made a mistake there, as Fargo hoped to demonstrate shortly.

"Faster, little bunny!" the killer chortled, and began counting out loud. He did not start with one. He started at ten, and counted quickly, not slowly.

Martha remonstrated with her offspring until Leroy snapped, "Shut up, Ma! I'm having fun." Then he ignored her.

An extra urgency galvanized Fargo to greater effort. It was not just his life at stake. He had to warn Sergeant Macon about the rattler in Macon's saddlebags. Every minute, every second, was critical.

"You're almost there!" Leroy hollered, and cackled. "You make a fine bunny, scout! All that's missing are the long ears!"

Another hop, and yet one more, and Fargo was in among the trees. A small pine barred his way and he veered to the left to go around it. But changing direction proved more difficult than he had counted on. He came down on the edge of his boots, not on the flat of the soles, and lost his balance. Tottering, he frantically sought to stay upright and just barely succeeded. Ten feet more he covered. Twenty feet. By then he was sure Leroy couldn't see him. Stopping, he threw himself onto his side. Quickly, he pried at the rope around his ankles, wriggling and tugging so he could slide the loops high enough to permit him to slide his fingers into his right boot.

The hilt of the Arkansas toothpick molded to Fargo's palm. He always kept the doubled-edged blade honed to razor sharpness. The knife made short shrift of the ankle rope. Standing, he reversed his grip and was about to saw at the wrist rope when Leroy called out to him.

"Ready or not, here I come!"

Fargo ran. He hugged the bottom of the hills, where the going was easier. As he ran, he cut at the rope, gripping the hilt firmly so as not to drop it.

Mocking laughter followed him but it did not last long. Suddenly Leroy stopped laughing, and there was an enraged "What's this?" He had found the ankle rope, Fargo guessed. "How in the hell? Where did you get a knife, scout? You're cheating, and I don't like cheaters!"

Fargo smiled grimly. If he had his way, the son of a bitch was in for a few more surprises. He rounded a bend, nearly whooping for joy when the wrist rope parted.

This time he did not let it lie where it fell. He tossed it into high weeds. Although Leroy would take it for granted that his hands were free, there was no sense in confirming they were.

Fargo ran smoothly on, flowing over the ground with a speed only an experienced frontiersman could achieve. He was a human buck, vaulting obstacles with deceptive ease. He was a human fox, choosing the hardest patches of ground so as to leave fewer tracks. Mostly, though, he was a human panther, determined to become the hunter instead of the hunted, and slay his quarry by any means necessary.

"Where are you?" Leroy bawled in mild frustration. The game had turned serious and he did not like it. His lark was now deadly.

Serves him right, Fargo thought. All those people Leroy had murdered, all those children. Killing men and women was bad enough. Killing children was unspeakably vile. It was as low as anyone could stoop, the most heinous of crimes. Hanging was too good for him. If there was any justice in the world, Leroy would suffer, and suffer horribly, before he died.

Fargo would like to see to it that he did. But he must not give in to emotion. He must stay clearheaded. If an opportunity presented itself to end Leroy's life, whether Leroy suffered greatly or not, he must take advantage of it. The important thing was to stay alive.

A dry twig crunched loudly to Fargo's rear. The underbrush crackled. Leroy was running. Instead of tracking him, Leroy had divined the general direction of his flight and was in swift pursuit.

Fargo could use that against him. He swept around another hill and passed through a stand of saplings. A thicket loomed on his left. Without hesitation he dived into it as he would into a pool of water, heedless of the branches that tore at his buckskins and his face. Twisting on his shoulder, he held the toothpick poised to attack if it came to that.

Heavy breathing heralded Leroy. The younger man swept around the hill, his legs churning. He was not looking at the ground. He did not glance right or left. He stared hard straight ahead, hoping to spot Fargo, the Henry clutched in his right hand. The promise of death blazed in his eyes.

Fargo lay still until the thud of Leroy's boots faded.

Standing, he ripped loose of the clinging thicket. He had a choice to make. He could play cat and mouse there in the forest, or he could do the last thing Leroy might expect him to do, and get his hands on a better weapon.

Whirling, Fargo flew back the way he had come. It turned out to be farther than he had realized, and it was some minutes before he spied the cabin off through the trees. Not until he burst into the open did he see that the front door was wide open. The Ovaro was where he had left it. His rope lay on the ground. So, too, much to his delight, did his Colt. Halting, he scooped it up. Only then did it occur to him that Martha was not there.

Fargo said her name, but not too loudly. "Are you inside?" When she did not answer, he stepped to the doorway, and froze.

Martha Barstow lay on her back near the table. Twin pools of glistening scarlet spread outward from near her hands. Beside the left one was the butcher knife, the big blade smeared red.

"No!" Fargo exclaimed, and dashed over. He grimaced at the deep cuts in her wrists. She had slashed them clear down to the bone. To stanch the flow would do no good. She had already lost too much blood. Squatting, he bent over her. "Martha?" he said softly. From her pallor and her stillness, he half expected she was already dead, but she blinked.

"You're still alive? Thank God."

"Why?" Fargo said softly.

"Need you ask? He's broken me. Broken my heart, my spirit." Martha smiled wanly. "Don't look so sad. It's how I want it to end. And there's not much pain. Not much pain at all."

"You should have waited."

"For what? For either him or you to come back? I couldn't stand the thought of it not being you. I want

136

him dead. My own son. I've wished he was dead for a very long time, but only today did I want him dead more than I ever wanted anything in my whole life."

Fargo put a hand on her shoulder. "I'm sorry."

"For what? I've thought about taking my life many times. But until today I was too much of a coward to do it."

"You are braver than you think."

"What a wonderful liar you are. I have never been brave. Not once my whole life long. If I had been, I would have done what needed doing. I should have strangled him when he was seven."

"You're his mother," Fargo said.

"So? I'm the mother of a monster. Thank God there aren't many like him, or where would we all be?"

Her voice was fading. The two pools had formed a pond, with Fargo and Martha at the center.

"The worst thing is all those people. All those lives I am to blame for because I have been so weak."

"Your son is to blame, not you," Fargo corrected her.

"You sweet man. I am sorry for all you have gone through on account of my son." Martha fell silent.

Fargo lightly pressed a finger to her neck and felt a weak pulse. "Is there anything I can get you? Water? A blanket?"

"The only thing I want is for you to do what I should have done," Martha replied. "End it. Please. No one else must suffer. Do I have your word?"

"You have it."

Contentment relaxed Martha's features. "It's strange. I feel like I am drifting off to sleep. It's rather nice."

Fargo glanced out the front door. As yet there was no sign of Leroy, but he was bound to make a beeline for the cabin once he realized he had been duped. "Is there a rifle in the house?"

Martha was slow to respond. "What was that? A rifle? No. He wouldn't let me have a gun." Tears formed and trickled from the corners of her eyes. "He was such a darling baby. He hardly ever cried or gave me a lick of trouble. I had such hopes for him. Such high hopes."

Fargo was anxious to confront Leroy but he would be damned if he would leave her there alone.

"I remember the first steps he took. And his first word. I was feeding him and he looked at me with those adorable eyes of his and said, 'Ma.' I was so happy, I cried."

"Martha—" Fargo said.

"I know. Indulge me. It won't be long."

Fargo was keeping one eye on the door. He saw the Ovaro lift its head and prick its ears toward the woods. "No, it won't," he said.

"Will you do me one more favor?" Martha unexpectedly asked, and told him what it was.

To Fargo it seemed a waste. "Are you sure?"

"I would rather it was final," Martha said. "Like erasing chalk on a blackboard. Will you do it for me?"

Fargo nodded, but apparently her vision was failing because she asked the question again, more urgently. "I will do it," he said aloud.

"Thank you." Martha's body went limp and she let out a long sigh. "This world sure is a peculiar place." With that, she expired.

Using the tips of two fingers, Fargo closed her eyes. He rose to run to the door and slipped on the slick blood. Lunging for the table, he stayed upright. On the counter was a frayed towel. It served to clean the blood off his boots. Skirting the pool, he made it to the door just as a figure materialized at the tree line. Instantly, he drew back so he would not be spotted.

"Ma?" Leroy called.

Fargo fingered the Colt. He needed Barstow to come closer.

"Ma? Can't you hear me? I need to know if it's safe. That coyote got loose and he could be anywhere."

Taking off his hat, Fargo put an eye to the jamb. Leroy had ventured a few steps into the clearing but he was not quite close enough for a sure shot.

"Ma? Damn it, answer me!"

Fargo had an idea. He holstered the Colt and went to Martha. "I know you wouldn't hold this against me," he said to the body, and proceeded to drag it by the hands over to the door. Careful not to show himself, he slid her forward until her head and part of one shoulder could be seen.

"Ma!" Leroy advanced several strides. "What's wrong? Did he hurt you?"

Gripping an elbow, Fargo moved Martha's arm to give the impression she was beckoning.

Leroy came closer. Only a few yards, though. Then he stopped, wariness written plain on his face. "Ma? Why don't you answer me?" Suddenly he snapped the Henry to his shoulder and took aim. Not at the doorway but at the Ovaro. "You're in there, aren't you, scout? Show your miserable hide, damn you, or I'll shoot your horse."

Fargo wanted to kick himself for not moving the pinto. He had not let it die before; he would not let it die now.

"I mean it!" Leroy snarled. "Come out where I can see you, and bring my ma!"

"Hold on!" Fargo shouted. Slipping his hands under Martha's arms from behind, he hoisted her as high as his chest. He held her in front of him so as not to soak his buckskins with the blood drenching her dress. With her body as a shield, he sidled into the doorway.

A string of oaths exploded from Leroy. His faced became a livid red. Taking a few more steps, he bawled, "Ma! What have you done to her, you bastard?"

Fargo turned one of her arms so Leroy could see her wrist. "Don't blame me. Blame yourself."

"No!" Leroy cried. "No! No! No! No! No!" Tilting his head back, he shrieked a banshee wail. The cry was torn from the core of his being, and when he stopped, he swayed as if dizzy. But only for a second or two. Then he glowered at Fargo. "I won't let them speak ill of her now that she's gone!" he roared. "Do you hear me? I'll kill every last one of them before I let them do that!"

Fargo was unsure who Barstow was referring to. "Don't you want to bury her before you do anything else?"

Without warning, Leroy began working the Henry's lever like a madman while screeching, "I'll bury you, you son of a bitch!"

Caught flat-footed, Fargo dived to the right, bearing Martha with him. Lead struck the jamb, the floor. With a fleshy *thwack,* two slugs jarred Martha's body. More peppered the cabin as Fargo released her and scrambled over to the log wall. As he rose into a crouch the firing stopped. He waited for Leroy to holler or do something, but a profound quiet had fallen.

Fargo figured that Leroy would wait out there for him to show himself, or maybe try to pick him off through a window. Which made him all the more surprised when hoofbeats proved him wrong. The sound came from the rear of the cabin, and rapidly dwindled.

Suspicious of a trick, Fargo moved to the door. Shoving his hat back on, he risked a peek. The Ovaro was grazing unconcernedly. As incredible as it seemed, Leroy had lit a shuck. But to where? Fargo wondered.

The killer's last words echoed in his head: *I'll kill every last one of them before I let them do that!*

Fargo stiffened. Springing to the Ovaro, he forked leather. He flicked the reins and resorted to his spurs.

Lives were at stake.

Leroy was on his way to Jaflyn—to wipe out every last soul.

17

Fargo came on the first body sooner than he expected. He was half a mile beyond the hills, riding hell-bent for leather, when he spied what appeared to be an untended horse up ahead. As he drew nearer he saw that the animal was cropping grass near a long, low shape on the ground.

It was Sergeant Macon.

Vaulting from the saddle while the Ovaro was still in motion, Fargo ran to the stricken trooper's side. Kneeling, he rolled Macon over. The bite was on Macon's right hand, the fang marks tiny red pinpoints that might easily be overlooked by someone unaware of the situation. As he examined them, Macon groaned.

"Jim?" Fargo said, shaking him. "Can you hear me?"

Macon opened his eyes and gazed weakly about. "Fargo? Where am I? What happened?"

"You don't remember?"

"I was on my way to Mankato, wasn't I?" Macon said confusedly. "I reached back into my saddlebags for my pipe and tobacco and something stung me."

"*Bit* you," Fargo set him straight. "Leroy Barstow stuck a rattlesnake in your saddlebags."

"What?" Sergeant Macon tried to rise but only made it as high as his elbows before he fell back. "Damnation. I feel as weak as a damn kitten."

"You're lucky to be alive." In Fargo's estimation the only thing that had saved him was the fact that the snake's fangs had not gone all the way in but only broken the skin, no doubt because Macon had jerked his hand away at the contact.

"I thought you were staying with the woman in case the son came back," Macon rasped.

"I was, he did, and now I'm on my way to Jaflyn to stop him from killing everyone. Or at least, that's where I think he's headed."

Sergeant Macon made another effort to rise and this time sat up. "Go on ahead, then. I'll be fine." But his sagging head and the way he mumbled belied his claim.

Fargo was torn. He could make better time alone, but the venom in the sergeant's system might cause a relapse. "We'll go together."

"Think of all those people," Macon objected. "I might not be up to a long, hard ride."

"I didn't take you for puny," Fargo chided. "Here. Lean on me." He helped Macon to stand and braced him when Macon started to pitch forward. "Can you make it or do I leave you for the coyotes and buzzards?"

Fierce determination hardened the soldier's face. "I'm not dead yet, you ornery cuss." He took a tentative step, then another, then shrugged loose of Fargo's grasp and stood on his own. "Maybe I am up to it, after all."

"Then let's quit jawing and fan the breeze." Fargo watched closely as Macon turned to his mount and reached for the saddle horn. Macon had to lift his leg twice before his boot snugged the stirrup. Clenching his jaw, Macon climbed on. Quickly, Fargo did the same.

Beads of sweat dotted Macon's face as they brought their mounts to a trot. Fargo continued to watch closely, ready to rein in close if Macon passed out, but the big sergeant was made of iron inside as well as outside. The longer they rode, the more like his old self Macon became. The effects of the snakebite were gradually wearing off.

Midway between the junction and Jaflyn they came on a buckboard stopped in the middle of the road. The team lay in their traces, the horses cored through their heads. A woman was sprawled across the seat, part of her temple blown away. A man, evidently her husband, was on the ground by the front wheel. A slug through the mouth had claimed his life.

"Leroy isn't waiting until he gets to town," Sergeant Macon said.

Grimly, they rode on. A quarter of a mile brought them to another body, an older man, a farmer, by his clothes. The tracks in the dust told the story. The farmer had been riding out of town and had the ill luck to meet Leroy coming the other way. They had stopped next to one another. Maybe words had been exchanged. Something happened to cause the farmer to wheel his mount and race off, but he had only gone a score of yards when Leroy shot him between the shoulder blades. The farmer fell, his horse ran on, and Leroy had resumed riding toward Jaflyn.

"He's killing everyone he meets," Fargo declared. Even horses. They soon came on the dead man's mount, equally dead. "Do you still intend to take him alive?"

"Need you ask?"

Fargo wished Macon would change his mind. Obeying orders was well and good but there was such a thing as going too far. Stubbornness was a poor substitute for common sense.

Buildings hove into view. No one was moving about but Fargo had not seen anyone moving about the last time so the absence of people might not be as sinister as it appeared. Nonetheless, he drew his Colt.

Sergeant Macon noticed. "You are not to shoot unless I say so. Otherwise, stay here and I'll go in alone."

"We'll do this your way," Fargo said. *For the time being.*

On their last visit Fargo had been struck by how closely Jaflyn resembled a cemetery. It was even more so now. Nothing stirred. Not so much as a cat. They drew rein at the north end of the empty, dusty street.

Macon had shucked his carbine. "Where is everyone?"

Gigging their mounts forward, they were almost to the frame house where Tommy Hinmet lived when a faint cry reached them.

"Help! Help us, please!"

Fargo was first to swing down and first through a gap in the hedge. The front door was open but he did not barrel in. "Tommy? Is that you?"

"He's shot us."

No need to ask who the boy meant. Darting inside, Fargo nearly tripped over a small crumpled figure. Tommy was on his back, his mouth flecked with dark drops. One look at his chest was sufficient.

"My ma," Tommy said. "In the kitchen."

Sergeant Macon hurried past. He was only gone a few moments. When he came back, he shook his head.

Tommy's spark was almost extinguished. "It's the Devil," he got out. "He's going from door to door. I heard shooting and shouting and opened ours, and there he was." The boy coughed more drops. "He never gave me a chance. He—"

There would be no more. Fargo slowly rose. "And you *still* want to take the bastard alive?"

"Quit asking that. I have a job to do." Macon stalked out. He got as far as the threshold. A shot boomed. Snapping sideways, Macon grabbed at his left shoulder and ducked back inside. "That's what I get for being so careless," he grunted.

Staying low, Fargo sprang to the doorway. The street was still empty. Or almost. On the boardwalk in front of the millinery lay a large yellow dog, its jaw half shot off.

"I think it missed the bone." Sergeant Macon had unbuttoned a couple of buttons and was lightly poking the wound. He twisted partway around. "Did the slug go clean through?"

"Yes," Fargo confirmed. "It's not bleeding much, but you should let me bandage it."

"And have the deserter get away?" Macon shook his head. "Nothing doing. It can wait." He edged to the doorway. "Private Barstow! Can you hear me?"

Fargo was mildly surprised when Leroy answered, since it gave them some idea of where he was.

"You're still alive, Sergeant? Damn. My aim must be off." Leroy was moving as he hollered. "What do you want?"

"I'm giving you this one last chance to give yourself up. I promise no harm will come to you while you are in my custody."

Leroy's familiar cackle was wafted on the wind. "And people call *me* crazy! If you want me so bad, Sergeant, you'll have to come and get me."

More to himself than to Leroy, Sergeant Macon vowed, "That is exactly what I am going to do."

Before Fargo could say anything, Macon was out the door and racing for the hedge. He made it a heartbeat ahead of lead blasted his way, and flattened.

Leroy laughed and called out, "I like you, Sergeant. I truly do. Do you want to know why?"

Macon did not respond. He was crawling toward the south corner of the hedge, using his good arm for leverage.

"No? Well, I'll tell you anyway. I like you because I get to kill you more than once. You survived the rattler, and I know I hit you a minute ago. So by

146

all means, come after me. I can't wait to kill you a third time.''

Fargo had lingered long enough. Turning, he ran along the hall to the kitchen. The back door opened onto a small enclosed yard with more clods of dirt than grass. Rather than risk having the rusty gate hinges squeak, he vaulted the picket fence and sprinted past the rear of building after building until he came to the one he was sure must be the general store.

Fargo tried the back door. Normally, in small settlements like Jaflyn, no one ever locked the doors. The store's owner, Ira Spivey, was no exception. The door opened with only the slightest of sound, and Fargo slipped within.

A long, shadowed hall led to the front. The first doorway Fargo passed was to a storeroom. The same with the second. The third was Spivey's living quarters; a small room with a bed, a dresser, and a lamp, nothing more.

The door into the store proper was closed. Hunkered on the balls of his feet, Fargo cracked it an inch. All he could see was the back of the counter. Slowly opening the door wide enough for him to snake through, he crabbed to the end of the counter.

The quiet of a tomb prevailed. Fargo could hear a clock ticking. He poked his head past the counter and bit off an oath.

A few feet away lay Ira Spivey. His broken cane was beside him. The kindly old man had been shot five or six times, his frail chest virtually riddled. In addition, his face had been kicked in. Bits of teeth had dribbled from his mouth and sprinkled his chin. His nose was as flat as paper.

Fargo had never wanted to kill anyone as much as he did Leroy Barstow. The youth was a living example of all that was despicable and depraved in human nature. How someone so vicious could be born to a woman as gentle and decent as Martha Barstow was a mystery Fargo could not fathom. Some things in life were like that. They made no sense. They just *were*, and had to be dealt with accordingly.

Rising as high as the countertop, Fargo prowled an aisle toward the front. Merchandise was strewn over the floor. A vase and several cups had been smashed to bits. He avoided the pieces so as not to have them crunch underfoot.

The front door hung open, admitting a shaft of sunlight. Fargo avoided showing himself. He did not step near the wide window. If Leroy was in a building on the other side of the street, he could easily see in.

On elbows and knees, Fargo crabbed to just below the sill. Removing his hat again, he peeked out. The street was still deserted. In addition to the dead dog, Fargo caught sight of a leg jutting from the door of the feed and grain.

It was unlikely anyone was still alive. The notion that one man could massacre an entire town seemed preposterous, but Jaflyn's total population amounted to no more than two dozen souls, a good portion women. For Leroy, slaying them was akin to picking off pigeons on a barn roof.

Fargo saw no trace of Sergeant Macon. He was about to crawl to the door when his attention was drawn to the millinery. A shape had flitted across the window. He caught no more than a glimpse. Whether it was Macon or Barstow or someone else was impossible to tell.

Suddenly a gun thundered. Another answered. The shots came from inside the millinery. Only the two, and then silence.

Fargo waited for someone to appear but no one did. Several minutes of not knowing were all he could bear. He went out the door in a rush, the Colt cocked, his finger curled around the trigger. Zigzagging across the street, he gained the overhang without being shot at. The door was closed. He solved that with his boot. Diving headlong, he rolled as he hit and came up primed for violence. But no one was there. The shop smelled of perfume and flowers, befitting its female clientele.

Fargo had his choice of a flight of stairs to the second floor and a door at the back. He went up the stairs three at a bound. At the top he came on the owner, a middle-aged woman with a crimson stain on her bosom. Her mouth gaped in the scream she had voiced as she lay dying.

Rage coursed through Fargo. He would not let himself rest until he had put an end to Leroy once and forever.

Thankfully, the bedroom contained no more bodies. Fargo hurried back down and was only a few steps from the bottom when he noticed the door was open. It had not been open when he went upstairs.

Between the door and the stairs was a mannequin draped in a dress in progress. Two long leaps carried Fargo behind it. When no shots crashed, he charged forward, only to stop cold when he saw a callused hand and a uniform sleeve poking from the doorway. The Colt level, Fargo stepped over the outflung arm.

Sergeant Macon was on his side, his back to the wall. The third button from the top was gone, a bullet hole in its place. The size showed it was an exit hole, not an entry wound. Blood oozed copiously. Beside him lay his carbine.

"Macon?" Fargo touched his shoulder.

The sergeant opened his eyes and mustered a regretful smile. "I have had bad luck before, but nothing like this."

"How?" Fargo asked.

"I forgot to watch my back. Don't make the same mistake." Macon coughed, and winced. He did not have long left. "It might interest you to know I have changed my mind. You don't need to take Barstow alive."

"I never intended to," Fargo informed him.

Sergeant Macon's chuckle turned into a death rattle. His last words, choked out, were "Avenge me. Avenge all of them."

"You can count on it," Fargo told the corpse.

18

Fargo helped himself to the sergeant's carbine and ammo pouch. He verified there was a cartridge in the chamber, then moved toward the entrance. He was about two-thirds of the way across the room when the wide front window dissolved in a sparkling shower of bits and fragments of shattered glass. Simultaneously, he heard the thunder of three swift shots from the Henry.

Throwing himself prone, Fargo shielded his head and face. Slivers stung his hands, cheek, and neck, drawing tiny pricks of blood. Before the echoes of the shots had faded he was up off the floor. He figured that Leroy expected him to use the door. Instead, the carbine held crosswise in front of him and his right arm over his eyes, he crashed through what was left of the shattered window.

A bleat of surprise pinpointed Barstow, in a gap between two buildings across the street.

Snapping the carbine to his shoulder, Fargo fired. He rushed his shot and paid for his mistake. The slug bit into the corner of a building, missing the young killer by a handbreadth.

Leroy, startled, whirled and bolted.

Fargo gave chase, reloading as he ran, veering to the left so as not to frame himself in the gap and be an inviting target. His shoulder to the wall, he risked a peep. At the other end of the gap the Henry spat smoke and lead. Fargo jerked back and once again was stung by flying slivers, only this time they were slivers of wood.

"Did I nick you, scout?" Leroy gleefully hollered. "There's more lead where that came from! Come and get some!"

Sinking onto a knee, Fargo banged off a shot. But his quarry darted from view a split second before he squeezed the trigger.

"Is that the best you can do?" Leroy shouted. "I can't say much for your aim. Better luck next time!"

That infernal laugh was grating on Fargo's nerves. He began replacing the spent cartridge.

"What's the matter?" Leroy yelled. "Cat got your tongue?"

"Go to hell," Fargo said, and regretted it the moment he closed his mouth. He must not give Barstow the satisfaction.

"Touchy, aren't you?" Leroy responded. "By the way, how is your friend? That broad back of his made a fine bull's-eye."

So will your face, Fargo wanted to say, but didn't.

"No comment? No threats? I must say, for a scout you are a powerful disappointment. Most of the others I met loved to hear themselves talk. How is it that you're so different?"

Sinking onto his stomach, Fargo wedged the carbine's stock firmly to his shoulder and sighted down the barrel. But Leroy did not show himself. Fargo waited, hoping the other would make a fatal blunder.

Leroy Barstow had a habit of doing the unexpected. He did it again now. Barely a minute had gone by when hooves drummed to the south. Rising, Fargo raced to the end of the street. The killer was galloping off! Bent low over the saddle, Leroy glanced back, grinned, and waved.

Fargo took deliberate aim. Barstow was still within range. He took a deep breath and held it to steady his aim. Another few heartbeats, and he would rid the world of a vile menace.

Suddenly Leroy swung onto the side of his horse so that only part of an arm and leg were showing. Fargo shifted the carbine's sights to the leg. If he could hit it, Leroy might tumble. He was about to fire when something tugged at his buckskin pant leg.

Fargo glanced down to find, of all things, a gray kitten. It plucked at his pants with its claws while voicing a soft meow. "Go away." Fargo again went to shoot but the few seconds of distraction had proven costly.

Leroy was out of range. He had made good his escape.

Fargo indulged in a rare swearing spree. Barstow had more luck than ten men. But Fargo was not about to give up. He would see it through to the end—either Barstow's death, or his own.

Turning, Fargo gave a certain whistle. At the north end of the street, the Ovaro pricked its ears and came trotting toward him.

The kitten would not leave Fargo's pant leg alone. Bending, he patted it on the head. "Get lost, runt." He nudged it with his boot but all it did was playfully swat at his toe.

The Ovaro came to a stop. Fargo slid the carbine into the saddle scabbard, gripped the saddle horn, and gave Jaflyn a last look. With all the shooting, someone should have come to investigate. That no one had proved beyond any shred of doubt that Leroy had accomplished what he set out to do. The kitten might be the only thing left alive. Fargo looked down.

Tail swishing, the kitten had sat and was staring up at him. It uttered a tiny mew.

"There's just you and me," Fargo said. He went to

climb on, then paused. "Hell," he said gruffly, and stooping, he scooped the kitten into his arms and held it close to his chest. It didn't struggle. Indeed, it seemed quite pleased, and rubbed its head against his hand.

"Stupid cat," Fargo muttered. Mounting, he jabbed his spurs.

A mile fell behind him, two miles, three. The rolling farmland stretched to the horizon in all directions. Fargo was alert for sign that Leroy had left the road but he did not find any.

The next settlement, to the best of Fargo's recollection, was Cotterville, ten to twelve miles on. Larger than Jaflyn, it boasted a population of more than fifty. It also had a tavern.

The day gave way to the murk of twilight and twilight gave way to the ink of night. The kitten was curled up inside Fargo's shirt, sound asleep. He could feel it purring. The sensation was oddly soothing. But he refused to grow attached to the thing. With all the wandering he did, he had no room in his life for a pet.

Presently the lights of Cotterville appeared. Fargo slowed. Leroy might be waiting for him, hiding in ambush. Accordingly, Fargo reined off the road and circled around the town to approach from the south. He did not use the main street. Stopping under an oak at the outskirts, he tied the reins, drew his Colt, and padded to the rear of the structures on the right side of the street.

As he had done in Jaflyn, Fargo did here, moving past building after building until he came to the back of the tavern. If Leroy wasn't lying in ambush, the tavern was where he would be.

The back door was not bolted. Fargo cautiously advanced along a well-lit hall until he came to a kitchen. A man in a white apron was stirring soup in a pot. He gaped at the Colt and blurted, "If you've come to rob us, we don't keep much money handy."

"I'm after a killer," Fargo said, and described Leroy Barstow. "Has he taken a room for the night?"

"I wouldn't know. I've been back here. The person to ask is Mary Becker. She runs the place."

"Where can I find her?"

"Where she always is. Out front. But you better not wave that six-shooter at her. She keeps a scattergun under the counter."

"I'm obliged."

Voices and laughter warned Fargo the tavern was doing a brisk business. Apparently the locals were fond of the food. Or maybe the whiskey had something to do with it, for Fargo swore he smelled liquor before he came to a curtain that served as a partition. He moved it just wide enough to peer out.

Straight ahead was the front door, and near it a counter. To the right spread a dining area. Five of the six tables were occupied. To the left was a fireplace and several chairs for lounging. Behind the counter, scribbling in a ledger, was a striking redhead in a lime green dress. Under different circumstances, Fargo would have given her a lot more attention. But at the moment he had only Leroy Barstow on his mind, and Barstow was not anywhere to be seen.

Wary as a wolf, Fargo dipped the Colt into its holster and crossed to the counter. He noticed a door in a dark nook beyond the fireplace.

The woman with the luxurious red mane glanced up. A tentative smile curled her cheery red lips. "Where the devil did you sprout from?"

"I'm looking for someone." Fargo again provided a verbal sketch of Leroy Barstow. "Did he stop here to eat, by any chance?"

"The gent you described did more than that," the redhead said. "After he ate he took a room."

Fargo was dumbfounded. Leroy had wiped out an entire town, yet had the gall to rest up for the night not twenty miles away. It was all the more surprising because Leroy had to know he would come after him. Why, then, had Leroy made catching him so easy? Something was not quite right.

"I'm Mary Becker," the vision of loveliness was saying. "I own this tavern. Might I ask what your business is with my guest?"

"I aim to kill him."

To her credit, Mary was not shocked. She calmly looked him up and down and commented, "You don't appear to be insane, so I trust you have a good reason."

Fargo told her. All of it. Every grisly detail. It had the desired effect.

"Dear God in heaven. Maybe you should let me send for the sheriff. I can have him here by noon."

"Barstow will be gone by then," Fargo pointed out. "I might never have a better chance than right now."

"Can I help in any way?"

Fargo liked this woman. She had nerve, and savvy, and she filled out her dress in all the enticing places. "Too dangerous," he said. "Just tell me which room he's in, and if anyone is in rooms next to his." Walls were notoriously poor lead-stoppers, and Fargo would rather not send a bystander into the hereafter if he could help it.

"You go through there," Mary said, pointing at the nook. "He specifically asked for the room at the far back. The rooms nearest his are empty. An older couple has taken the first room, but at the moment they are out on a stroll."

Nodding, Fargo turned to go, but she put a warm hand on his.

"Be careful, hear? I realize we hardly know each other, but it would please me considerable to sit down and have a coffee with you, after."

"Count on it." Fargo steeled his mind against admiration of her bosom, and crossed to the door. Once again he drew the Colt. The hall was well lit. Five doors were on one side, spaced twenty feet apart. He crept past the first four, careful not to jangle his spurs. He pressed his ear to the fifth. All was quiet within. He gingerly tried the latch, and slowly pushed. Thankfully, the hinges didn't creak. A chair appeared. A small dresser was in one corner. The bed was near a window, the quilt as smooth as glass. A lit lamp on the dresser testified that Barstow had been there and gone.

A door garnered Fargo's interest. Gliding over, he wrenched it open to find an empty closet.

"One twitch and you're dead."

Resisting an impulse to spin around, Fargo transformed to stone. "The window," he said, disgusted with himself.

"The window," Leroy Barstow confirmed. "I reckon you feel mighty stupid along about now. Put the hogleg down, reach for the ceiling, and you get to live a little longer."

The skin between his shoulder blades burned as Fargo complied.

"You can turn around, scout. But do it nice and slow."

The window was open about six inches. Crouched outside was Leroy. He had the Henry to his shoulder, the barrel on the sill. That close, he could not miss if he tried. Chuckling, he raised the window one-handed. The Henry never wavered. Sliding one leg over and then the other, he straightened. "You walked right into my trap, you dunderhead. I didn't think it would be this easy."

Fargo was too mad at himself to respond.

"I figured you were after me, and I didn't want you dogging my footsteps all the way to South America." Leroy smirked. "Pretty clever of me, huh?"

"I've told others," Fargo stalled. "They'll send for the law."

"Let them," Leroy responded. "As soon as I blow windows in your skill, I'm lighting a shuck." His dark eyes glittered with sadistic delight as he put his cheek to the Henry. "Any last words, simpleton?"

Fargo girded to make a desperate lunge. He would die anyway, but he would do it fighting for his life.

Unexpectedly, Leroy's eyebrows pinched over his nose. He lowered the Henry a trifle. "What's that bulge under your shirt? I thought I saw it move."

Fargo had forgotten about the kitten. It was starting to stir. He opened his mouth to answer, and had a brainstorm. "It's my poke. Back pay and poker winnings."

"Your money? How much do you have?"

Desperate to keep Leroy interested, Fargo said, "I haven't counted it lately. There should be about four hundred dollars."

Leroy grinned at the news. "You don't say. And me with a paltry ten dollars to my name." He hefted the Henry. "Be a good scout, and take out your poke and toss it on the bed."

Fargo had two ways to do it. He could reach down under his shirt, or he could tug his shirt loose of his belt and reach up and under. He chose the former. It was less likely to agitate the kitten.

"Nice and slow," Leroy stressed.

"Just don't shoot." Fargo pretended to be cowed. The kitten was curled into a ball. Gently enfolding it in his hand, he began to ease it out.

Leroy licked his thin lips, and chuckled. "I was planning to rob the tavern but now I won't need to. Your poke should last me to New Orleans."

Fargo had the kitten almost out. Its eyes were open, and staring up at him adoringly. "Sorry," he said.

"About what?" Leroy asked.

In a blur of motion, Fargo whipped the kitten from under his shirt and threw it at Barstow's face. Even as the kitten left his fingers, he was diving toward the floor and his Colt. The Henry went off, the blast like thunder in the confines of the room, but the slug missed. Then Fargo was on his side, the Colt rising.

The kitten had sliced its claws into Leroy's cheeks and chin, and was hissing and biting in a frenzy of terror. Howling with rage, he swatted it aside.

Fargo fired as Leroy brought up the Henry, he fired as Leroy staggered, he fired as Leroy tripped over his own feet and sprawled against the bed. Incredibly, Leroy tried to rise, and Fargo fired once more, splattering his brains over the quilt.

In the sudden silence, the frightened kitten commenced mewing in panic. Going over, Fargo coaxed it from under the bed. The feline was none the worse for the battering it had received. He was fondling it when shouts and footsteps filled the hallway, and the next moment the door burst inward and in rushed a breathless Mary Becker. She barely gave the ghastly remains a glance. "Are you all right?"

"Just fine," Fargo said, and held out the kitten. "How would you like a pet?"

The next morning Fargo rode out of Cotterville. He had not gotten much sleep. Mary Becker had seen to that. She was insatiable in bed. Her lips had never stopped exploring every square inch of his muscled frame. Her fingers had caressed and stroked until he was fit to climb the walls. At the apex of their passion, with her pendulous breasts swaying above him and her riding him like he was a bucking mustang, Fargo gave himself over to a much-needed release.

Mary agreed to keep the kitten. She named it Skye.

Now, with the sun warm on his face, Fargo headed north, toward Jaflyn. He avoided the town. Instead, he swung west and by late afternoon arrived at the

Looking Forward!

**The following is the opening
section of the next novel in the exciting
Trailsman series from Signet:**

THE TRAILSMAN #304
DEATH VALLEY DEMONS

*Death Valley, California, 1861—where a
beautiful woman's treachery is as deadly as
an evil man's bullets.*

Skye Fargo heard the screams from a half mile off,
the high-pitched, almost feminine screams of a man
who was suffering the worst hurt in the world. Fargo
recognized the sound and knew it was pointless to
charge recklessly forward—the poor soul was past all
help.

The Trailsman, as some called Fargo, gigged his
black-and-white pinto stallion forward, his lake blue
eyes ever vigilant in the brittle afternoon sunlight and
furnace heat. He was traversing the upper end of Cali-

fornia's Death Valley, bearing toward Grapevine Canyon, which led down from the bleak and jagged mountains. Even down low in the dry creek wash he was following, winds whipped billows of sand, salt, and grit into his face and eyes.

More piercing, scalp-tingling screams from ahead raised the fine hairs on Fargo's arms. His nervous Ovaro whiplashed his head.

"Steady, old campaigner," Fargo calmed him, patting his neck. "He's about to go over the mountains, and we might too if we get careless."

Fargo was crop-bearded and wore fringed buckskin shirt and trousers, a tall, broad-shouldered man cut down to puny size by the sheer vastness of this sterile, 150-mile-long trough. Death Valley was walled by rock outcrops and surrounded on all sides by eastern California's merciless desert.

Fargo had only to climb a little higher, however, for a magnificent view of the Sierra Nevadas and their capes of dazzling white snow. But even a naked woman couldn't distract him from the horrific screams as he rode around a hill of black slag and two bodies eased into view.

The bridle-wise Ovaro stopped when Fargo tossed the reins forward. He swung his right foot over the cantle and landed light as a cat, sliding his brass-framed Henry from its boot. Fargo's sun-slitted eyes searched the rock-salt bed of the valley, but nothing moved except a few wisps of white-gauze cloud far overhead—there was nothing there that *might* move, for very little life existed in this wasteland.

"Aww, *Jee*-zus, it hurts!" screeched the one man who still clung to life. "Aww, God, it's pure fire!"

Both men had gotten in front of a bullet, the dead man a shot through the heart, the screamer a bullet low in the guts—even in cities with doctors a gut shot was fatal, much less out here in the most arid, barren region of the West. Each man had been shot at such close range his shirt caught on fire from the powder burn.

"Mister!" begged the dying man when he spotted Fargo. He was a young man with an honest face. "I know I'm dead. But, God A'mighty, some water first!"

"Sure wish I could do more, friend."

Fargo laid his Henry down and twisted the cap off his bull's-eye canteen. It was dangerously low, but Fargo couldn't deny even a dying man a drink.

"Who did this?" he asked as he knelt and cupped the man's head so he could drink.

Somewhere amid a string of curses and screams Fargo heard the curious words "mad dog." The dying man, face contorted with pain, clutched the Trailsman's sleeve.

"Woman!" he gasped. "She's . . . next. Killers . . . Christ all *mighty*, that hurts! Mister, *please* pop one in me."

Fargo could stand it no longer. Every instinct in him wanted to save life, not take it, but this suffering man could last for hours with each minute like a year in hell. The other man's weapon was missing, so Fargo shucked out his Colt and laid it near the man's hand. Only seconds after he started to walk away, the weapon spoke its piece.

"I hope I helped you," Fargo muttered, tasting the bitter bile of sudden anger as he returned for his revolver. No skunk-bit son of a bitch was making him play God like this and just riding off into the sunset.

Fargo searched both men and found letters written by Allan Pinkerton, the Chicago detective, identifying them as two operatives in his employ. That bothered

Fargo: Pinkerton men were generally brave and capable.

A woman . . . she's next . . . .

Fargo flinched hard when a gunshot split the lifeless silence, coming from Grapevine Canyon. He sprinted toward his stallion, even as two more shots echoed down the long valley known as Death.

Rena Collins felt fear hammering at her temples, but she tried to balance her conflicting impulses, knowing that one tiny mistake now meant brutal rape and death.

"What do you want from me, Mad Dog?" demanded Matt Conway, the silver-haired gent who had given Rena shelter only an hour earlier after her guards had been slain.

"Innocent as a nursery, ain't you?" replied one of the most brutal-looking men Rena had ever seen. "Did you think you could railroad Mad Dog Barton's kid brother to the gallows and live to brag about it?"

"Railroad? Christ sakes, your brother Lanny murdered a woman and her four-year-old daughter."

Rena, cowering in the loft of a small cabin, watched the brute's mouth curl into a sneer. "He did, didn't he?" Mad Dog said proudly. "That boy was hell on two sticks."

Rena gasped at this callow man, but Scotty McDaniels, the aging prospector who had saved her from Mad Dog and his gang, touched her arm in warning. His upper right thigh still oozed blood from a bullet one of the gang had put in it.

"Yessiree, Deputy Conway," Mad Dog went on, "you kill one of mine, I kill *all* of yours."

"Now simmer down. I retired last year. Hell, I

didn't kill your brother. I only brought him in for trial."

Mad Dog wore a richly embroidered sash with a pair of ivory-hilted, silver-mounted revolvers stuck into it. But he also held a shotgun, and Rena felt her skin crawl against her clothing when he thumbed back both hammers with a loud metallic *snick*.

"You *only* brought him in, Conway? Just a little Judas kiss, eh?"

Mad Dog's face, Rena told herself with a violent shudder, lived up to his sick name. His eyes, cunning and primitive, were two flat yellow disks, and when he talked or grinned, his lips pulled back to reveal teeth narrow and pointed like fangs.

Two more men had forced their way into the cabin with him: a small, furtive Mexican wearing rope sandals and a redheaded man whose hands were taking shocking liberties with Matt Conway's spinster daughter.

Mad Dog glanced around the cabin. It was simple but solid, with a puncheon floor, sawbuck kitchen table, and cast-iron cookstove. The one touch of elegance was a mirror in a bronze frame on the back wall. Rena flinched when Mad Dog drew his belt gun in a blur of speed and shot the mirror to shards.

"The first family living in Death Valley," Mad Dog sneered. "Thought you'd be safe here, hunh?"

Scotty again touched Rena in warning. His weather-seamed face looked white as a fish belly beneath his iron gray beard and mustache.

"Mad Dog, what's the point of this?" Conway tried to reason. "After all, your bother—"

"*I'm* the cock of this dung heap, not you. First you leave my brother dancing on air. Now you stand there and piss in my boots. That's no way to treat a man, 'specially when he's got you behind the eight ball."

"At least *please* leave my wife and daughter out of this!"

Mad Dog shook his shaggy head. "No can do, law dog."

"Please!" Conway repeated, his tone passionately earnest. "Don't punish them for my actions!"

"You mean, like this?"

Mad Dog swiveled toward Conway's wife and tweaked the gun's right trigger, the report deafening in the small cabin. The heavy buckshot cut Marsha Conway nearly in two and blew gobbets of bloody flesh all over her husband.

The retired deputy loosed a bray of grief, and the effort not to scream left a knot in Rena's throat. Hearing the terrible pain in Conway's voice, she felt the saline sting of tears.

"Please," the shattered man begged when Mad Dog pointed his double ten at Conway's shocked daughter, "not her, Mad Dog, *please.*"

"My side hurts from laughing so hard, star packer. You're gonna watch it, you shit heel *honest man*, and you're gonna see it forever in hell, printed on the back of your eyelids. This is for Lanny."

The prospector beside Rena carried a black-gripped Remington six-shooter tucked into his belt. She aimed an entreating gaze at it, but he shook his head in silent frustration.

"There's three below and one outside," he whispered. "They'll kill us both."

This time Mad Dog aimed deliberately high, nearly decapitating the Conway girl. The color ebbed from Rena's face as the horror of what she was watching sank in deep.

Matt Conway fell, sobbing, to the floor, driven mad by what he'd seen. Mad Dog finished him off with six bullets.

"The daughter's still warm," the redhead said. "Let's fetch the Kid inside so he can get him a poke. He likes it when they cooperate."

An unbidden noise of disgust in Rena's throat made all three men stare up toward the shadowy loft. She and Scotty already poured sweat from the stifling heat, but now it flowed like snowmelt.

"I think we just found our fine-haired sketchin' woman," Mad Dog announced. "And this one ain't goin' to waste before we kill her."

Yellow eyes gleaming with malice, a faint smile twitching one corner of his mouth, he headed toward the ladder.

Scotty had his six-shooter to hand now, ready to make his last stand. Rena's pulse leaped into her throat, and she eased a derringer from the pocket of her skirt. It was only a single shot, and she knew full well that lone bullet had her name on it.

"Heads up, boys!" a voice shouted from outside. "Rider comin' in loaded for bear!"

Rena, on the verge of firing a bullet through her right temple, heard a rapid drumbeat of hooves and felt hope soar within like the brush of wing tips against her heart.

"It's only one," the redhead scoffed. "We can snuff his wick easy."

"Good odds," Mad Dog agreed. "But if he gets away, he'll ride out of the valley now before we can stop him. Won't be long before the whole state knows who butchered the Conways. A tin star they might ignore, but not two women."

"I take your drift," the redhead agreed. "If we leave

167

Excerpt from DEATH VALLEY DEMONS

the cabin first, ain't nobody can get out of this valley without us knowing it. Besides, the Kid ain't no sharp-shooter, and this hombre might kill our mounts."

"Now you're whistlin'. We give him no chance to escape. Let's hop our horses and get out of here before this hombre sees us. Kid!"

"Yo!" shouted the voice outside.

"You're hid good in that pile of scree. Stay there and watch this jasper. Then pull foot and meet us at the usual place."

Rena, realizing all three men were racing to their horses, sagged to the floor, trembling too hard to stand up. The rider was so close now she could hear his bit ring rattling.

"Whoever this man is, Mr. McDaniels," Rena told the prospector, "he just saved our lives."

The prospector, gun in hand, peeked out through a break in the chinking. "Too soon to tack up bunting, miss. The one who just rode up looks like he could fight a cougar with a shoe, and he don't strike me as the type to let laws get in his way."